HOT SHOTS

Slocum picked up the shot glass and took a whiff of the aroma rising like mist after a gentle rain.

"Much obliged," Slocum said, starting to drink. The glass suddenly flew from his hand. Slocum spun, only to have a heavy hand push him back. His hand made it halfway to the butt of his six-shooter before he stopped. Eustace Harlow held him by the throat with his left hand and in his right was the small-caliber pistol usually slung under his arm.

"I ought to kill you where you stand, Slocum. How dare you interfere with a business transaction?"

Slocum considered his chances. Bent back over the bar the way he was, with Harlow's hand clenched on his throat, he wasn't able to get out of the way fast enough to survive. The banker had his pistol cocked and pointed at Slocum's face. Dodging a bullet or clearing leather with his own piece wasn't likely.

"You spilled my drink," Slocum said.

"What?" This took Harlow aback. In that instant of surprise, Slocum moved, bringing his hand up to the one gripping his throat. He twisted slightly against the banker's fingers to loosen the hold, pried away the choking fingers, then jerked hard on Harlow's thumb. The man yelped in pain and swung his pistol off-target. Slocum came erect, then applied pressure on the captive hand, forcing Harlow to his knees.

"Drop the gun," Slocum said. "Drop it now."

DON'T MISS THESE
ALL-ACTION WESTERN SERIES
FROM THE BERKLEY PUBLISHING GROUP

THE GUNSMITH by J. R. Roberts
Clint Adams was a legend among lawmen, outlaws, and ladies. They called him . . . the Gunsmith.

LONGARM by Tabor Evans
The popular long-running series about Deputy U.S. Marshal Long—his life, his loves, his fight for justice.

SLOCUM by Jake Logan
Today's longest-running action Western. John Slocum rides a deadly trail of hot blood and cold steel.

BUSHWHACKERS by B. J. Lanagan
An action-packed series by the creators of Longarm! The rousing adventures of the most brutal gang of cutthroats ever assembled—Quantrill's Raiders.

DIAMONDBACK by Guy Brewer
Dex Yancey is Diamondback, a Southern gentleman turned con man when his brother cheats him out of the family fortune. Ladies love him. Gamblers hate him. But nobody pulls one over on Dex . . .

WILDGUN by Jack Hanson
The blazing adventures of mountain man Will Barlow—from the creators of Longarm!

TEXAS TRACKER by Tom Calhoun
Meet J.T. Law: the most relentless—and dangerous—manhunter in all Texas. Where sheriffs and posses fail, he's the best man to bring in the most vicious outlaws—for a price.

JAKE LOGAN

SLOCUM AND THE WATER WITCH

J

JOVE BOOKS, NEW YORK

THE BERKLEY PUBLISHING GROUP
Published by the Penguin Group
Penguin Group (USA) Inc.
375 Hudson Street, New York, New York 10014, USA
Penguin Group (Canada), 90 Eglinton Avenue East, Suite 700, Toronto, Ontario M4P 2Y3, Canada
(a division of Pearson Penguin Canada Inc.)
Penguin Books Ltd., 80 Strand, London WC2R 0RL, England
Penguin Group Ireland, 25 St. Stephen's Green, Dublin 2, Ireland (a division of Penguin Books Ltd.)
Penguin Group (Australia), 250 Camberwell Road, Camberwell, Victoria 3124, Australia
(a division of Pearson Australia Group Pty. Ltd.)
Penguin Books India Pvt. Ltd., 11 Community Centre, Panchsheel Park, New Delhi—110 017, India
Penguin Group (NZ), Cnr. Airborne and Rosedale Roads, Albany, Auckland 1310, New Zealand
(a division of Pearson New Zealand Ltd.)
Penguin Books (South Africa) (Pty.) Ltd., 24 Sturdee Avenue, Rosebank, Johannesburg 2196,
South Africa

Penguin Books Ltd., Registered Offices: 80 Strand, London WC2R 0RL, England

This is a work of fiction. Names, characters, places, and incidents either are the product of the author's imagination or are used fictitiously, and any resemblance to actual persons, living or dead, business establishments, events, or locales is entirely coincidental.

SLOCUM AND THE WATER WITCH

A Jove Book / published by arrangement with the author

PRINTING HISTORY
Jove edition / December 2005

Copyright © 2005 by The Berkley Publishing Group.

ISBN: 0-515-14042-2

JOVE®
Jove Books are published by The Berkley Publishing Group,
a division of Penguin Group (USA) Inc.,
375 Hudson Street, New York, New York 10014.
JOVE is a registered trademark of Penguin Group (USA) Inc.
The "J" design is a trademark belonging to Penguin Group (USA) Inc.

PRINTED IN THE UNITED STATES OF AMERICA

10 9 8 7 6 5 4 3 2 1

1

Dust. Everywhere he looked there was nothing but dust and brown, sere grass that had once grown thick and verdant and waist high. John Slocum tried but couldn't remember when he had seen anything larger than a jackrabbit on the ride across the northern Wyoming prairie. The herds of buffalo were gone, ranging farther south and east hunting for water in a world that insisted on squeezing every drop of moisture from anything living.

Slocum mopped his brow, settled his bandanna around his neck again and then pulled it up to protect his nose and mouth from the choking dust. His Appaloosa whinnied in protest, but Slocum had his eyes on the Grand Tetons rising ahead, cool in the distance, promising high green meadows and water. Lakes. Rivers. Free-flowing water enough to dive into and drink and bathe in.

But first he had to reach those wondrous, purple-clad mountains. He kept his head down so the brim of his Stetson shaded his eyes from the blazing sun. Slocum had spent the better part of the spring ranging from Texas to Nebraska looking for work. The drought had seized the center of the country with a grip that refused to slacken. Cattle ranchers butchered their herds and farmers watched as insects dined on desiccated corn and wheat. He had considered stowing away on a Mississippi river boat heading southward to New Orleans and trying his luck there, but he had come by the sturdy Appaloosa now swaying gently under him in a card game and didn't have the heart to abandon the horse. He lacked enough money to bring it aboard a paddle wheeler so he lit out for the Oregon coast. It had been a month of Sundays since he'd see the green strip of land running along the Pacific Ocean, and he couldn't think of a better time to renew the acquaintance.

There might even be need of a wrangler on a stud farm.

Slocum didn't much care what job he got as long as he wasn't being burned to a cinder on his saddle under the blazing sun without a canteen sloshing full of water.

Doggedly riding, he made his way across the prairie until the land began sloping upward more and more into the foothills. He felt cooler wind whistling from the higher elevations and breathed a sigh of relief. He was getting to a spot where he could drink water and not have to worry if there'd be enough left for a second taste.

As he rode he began to notice other tracks in the dusty road. At first he was glad to see them because it meant he was heading toward a town where freighters stopped. Then he saw increasing signs that a wagon was in trouble. The right wheel appeared to wobble more and more as it had rattled up the slope. Then, he saw the wheel—but not the wagon.

The roadbed passed perilously close to a ravine. Slocum rode over and peered down into the sheer-walled arroyo and simply stared at the wreckage. There was no way in hell the driver could be alive. The wagon had crushed him as they had tumbled over the brink after the wheel came off.

A dozen thoughts flashed through Slocum's head, but he discarded them one by one and finally dismounted to do what common decency dictated. It was hot and dry, but he had to bury the man rather than let coyotes and buzzards dine on him. The drop-off was steep enough to force Slocum to look for another way down the ten-foot escarpment. He walked a hundred yards farther along the road, then found a ravine cutting through the bank where he could slip and slide down. As he neared the overturned wagon, he froze. At first he thought it was a trick of the wind. Then he heard the low moan coming from ahead.

"Hang on, I'm coming," he called. Slocum dropped to his knees beside the pinned driver, then saw that the man was very, very dead. Part of the wagon bed had dislodged and driven through the man's back, impaling him. Even if he hadn't been crushed by the weight of the wagon, the spear would have killed him instantly.

Slocum heard the moan again and got to his feet to look around. Half hidden in a deep trench a dozen paces off he saw a man's arm waving about weakly. He ran to the man and stared down at him. Eyelids fluttered open and bloodshot brown eyes stared up at him. Lips cracked from the heat and lack of water formed a single word.

Help.

"Come on, let's get out of the sun," Slocum said. He grunted as he heaved the man upright, then slung him over his shoulders. Stumbling along in the gravelly bottom of the ravine, Slocum returned to the wagon. A small amount of shade was created by the side of the wagon. Dropping his burden, Slocum arranged the man to lie as comfortably as he could out of the direct sunlight. He poked around in the spilled contents of the wagon and found a desert bag. The inch-long gash had allowed most of the water to leak out, but a mouthful remained. Slocum spilled it across the man's lips and brought him up with the first show of strength. This quickly faded when the man realized there was no more water.

"I'll get my canteen. Don't have much left but you can have what's there. Are we far from a town?"

The man made gurgling noises, realized he couldn't speak and then shook his head slowly.

"We'll make it. Don't go running off, hear?" Slocum saw the man's lips curl into a little smile. He trooped back to the road, fetched his canteen, resisted the impulse to take just a swig for himself, then returned to give the man all he had.

Some spilled down the man's chin, but Slocum got most of the water into the man's mouth.

"You didn't notice how your right wheel was coming loose?"

The man shook his head and croaked out, "Weren't thinkin' straight. Water. Not enough water. Been on trail for days."

"Don't get yourself all tuckered out," Slocum said. "Rest up. When it's closer to sundown, we'll start for town. Can we make it in an hour or two?" The man nodded, then slumped from exhaustion. Besides being badly dehydrated, the man had suffered many other injuries from the tumble down the steep embankment.

Knowing there wasn't anything he could do about either the lack of water or the man's injuries, Slocum curled up in the dubious shade and pulled his hat low to grab a few winks himself. When he awoke, the sun was dipping just under the summit of the distant Grand Tetons.

He pushed up his hat brim and looked at his patient, almost hoping the man had died. If anything, the sun-baked man had strengthened and had pulled himself into a more comfortable position.

"Thanks," the man croaked out. "You saved me for sure."

"We're not out of trouble yet," Slocum said, "unless we find some water. You drank all I had."

"Sorry," the man said, sounding as if he meant it.

"You heading into a town? Is there water ahead? How far?" Slocum had a million questions but these were foremost in his mind. He needed water as badly as the man he'd pulled out of the ravine.

The man nodded or so Slocum thought until he saw that he had passed out again. Grumbling, Slocum pushed erect and went to kneel beside the man. His pulse was strong, but he had passed out again from lack of water. Considering his options didn't leave Slocum with a powerful lot of choice. Getting his arm around the man, Slocum heaved him up and over his shoulders and staggered off to fetch his horse. The Appaloosa snorted in disgust at the notion of having to carry twice the weight.

Slocum wouldn't put the horse through that. He dropped the man belly down over the saddle and started walking down the road, trusting that the town wouldn't be too far. The cool breeze blowing in his face evaporated sweat fast and cooled him after a long day of heat. Less than two miles up the road he saw a signpost with the name "Campbell" scratched out and replaced with "Dehydration." Considering how sere the grass along the road appeared and the tiny clouds of dust he kicked up as he walked, Slocum thought that was probably a reasonable change of name.

Another mile along he came to a few deserted shacks, but a hundred yards farther he spotted a light in a window. He had plodded along from the site of the accident but now his step developed a spring to it as he neared the town—and water. His horse snorted and tossed its head as it scented the divine liquid.

The town of Dehydration—or Campbell as it once had been called—had seen better days, but Slocum hardly cared about the fate of a western Wyoming cow town. All he wanted was water. Giving his Appaloosa its head, the horse led him to a rain barrel with a lid secured on it. Slocum fumbled to get the top off. He plunged his head in, then scooped water until his own cottony mouth was moist. Then he fetched his canteen to fill it to give some to his miraculously still-living ward.

The canteen gurgled and bubbled as water flowed in. Slocum turned with the half-full canteen to give some to the man flopped over his saddle while his horse drank noisily.

"Hey, you there!" came the harsh call. "You're stealin' our water!"

"Dying of thirst," Slocum got out. His mouth and lips were better but he still felt the effects of his afternoon without water. "I can pay. Gold."

"Well, all right, but we'd as soon you lent a hand haulin' more. We gotta bring it in from a waterin' hole ten miles out on the prairie."

"Be glad to once I get my strength back."

"Who's that?" the man asked, edging closer and peering at the feebly stirring accident victim.

"Don't rightly know. Found him all bunged up. His wagon lost a wheel. Killed the driver and threw him out into the sun. He must have been there cooking for hours before I found him. Mighty tough to survive that long."

The man who had inquired moved closer, then grabbed a handful of hair and yanked to expose the face that had been pressed into a stirrup.

"Son of a bitch! This here's Marsh Campbell!"

Slocum saw how half the town came pouring out of their burrows, rushing over to see. He went to Marsh Campbell and started to give him some water from the canteen.

"Give that varmint so much as a drop of our water and I'll fill you full of holes." Slocum looked up and found himself staring down the huge bores of a double-barreled shotgun. The mountain of a man holding it wasn't kidding. And he wore a marshal's badge that reflected just enough light from a nearby house to let Slocum know he had stepped into a nest of rattlers.

"He hasn't had any water all day. He'll die without it."

"Let him." The marshal wasn't alone in this sentiment.

Slocum explained how he had come upon the wrecked wagon and taken Marsh Campbell to Dehydration.

"Those fools don't know when to quit," snarled the shadow-cloaked man.

"They certainly had no reason to keep water from a dying man, but they did. But I'm beginning to get a feel for why they're so angry if you're always this inhospitable." Slocum squared off, feet spread about shoulder-wide and his hand resting at his right hip. He wore his Colt Navy in a cross-draw holster and considered how fast he could get his iron out and blazing, even with the hidden man having the drop on him.

A tall, whipcord-thin man stepped from the shadows. He held a six-gun of his own aimed at Slocum's belly.

"You'd throw down on me? Even though I got you covered?"

"Bad manners is reason enough," Slocum said.

"You don't have the sense God gave a goose."

"Might be caused by being out in the hot sun, sharing what little water I have with Marsh Campbell here, and burying the man who was with him. Folks have poked shotguns in my belly and told me not to drink their water. Now you're being downright objectionable."

"Gus, Luke, go see if that's Marsh."

From behind Slocum came two armed men who pushed past him and dragged the passenger off Slocum's saddle. They eased him to the ground.

"Surely is, Mr. Campbell."

"Your son?" asked Slocum.

"Yeah."

"He's a damn sight more polite than his pa, but then he hasn't been able to talk and has been out of his head most of the time I've known him. Would he be as ornery if he had his fill of water?"

"Get out. You've got ten minutes to get the hell off my land before I order my men to fill you full of lead."

"He drank all my water. I want a canteen full for my trouble."

"You don't know what's best for you, do you, mister?"

"The water." Slocum's words hung in the air, razor-edged and warning of the death that would be unleashed if he didn't get his demand met.

"Gus, give him your canteen."

"Yes, sir," spoke up the larger, older of the men tending Marsh Campbell. He got to his feet and hurried off. Slocum remained alert for a trick. He was beginning to appreciate the animosity the townspeople had for the owner of the Circle C.

"Here, mister. It's only half full but—"

"That'll do him," Campbell said harshly.

"Let your son drink it," Slocum said, tossing the canteen to the man who still supported the younger Campbell where he lay on the ground.

Slocum swung into the saddle. The Appaloosa protested and then gave a snort and almost pranced out of the canyon. Slocum agreed. He couldn't leave soon enough, either.

2

Slocum rolled over, aching and tired and feeling as if he had been pulled through a knothole backward. He sat up and let his blanket fall away. The sun was barely poking over the eastern horizon and already it was hot. Too damned hot for someone without any water. Looking around, he saw how his Appaloosa foraged in vain for green grass or anything worth the effort of eating. Mouth like the inside of a cotton bale, Slocum got to his feet, drew his knife and began hacking at a prickly pear cactus.

Once he had a few pads cut free from the main plant, he started skinning the tough hide off, taking the spines with it. He was left with a sticky, milky pulp that he held out for his horse. The Appaloosa gratefully licked and then gulped at the prickly pear, seeking as much moisture from every pad as possible. Slocum worked for close to a half hour, feeding the abundant but bitter plant to his horse, then gnawed on some himself. The dampness trickled down his throat and tormented him more than it eased the thirst.

Since he had seen the river was dammed up and skeleton dry, he needed to find another source of water fast. After climbing to the highest nearby rock and spending the better part of a half hour studying the terrain with his field glasses, Slocum decided there wasn't any water to be had.

Except in Dehydration.

He considered his chances of getting back to the town and begging for some water. His last encounter with the townsfolk had been done in the dark. They might not recognize him, and without Marsh Campbell draped over the saddle, they might not even recognize as distinctive a horse as an Appaloosa. Slocum doubted any of that was possible, but he had no choice. He had to return to the unfriendly town.

He walked his horse a couple miles, then mounted when his legs began to buckle. By the time he reached Dehydration, he was nodding off in the saddle.

Only the sound of voices brought him around in time to keep him from riding clean through the town and back onto the Wyoming prairie he had crossed the day before.

"You look 'bout half past dead, mister," called the man sitting in front of the general store. "You care for a dipper of water?"

"That'd be a lifesaver," Slocum croaked out. He hardly recognized his own voice. "Don't know how I can repay you."

"Not too hard. We need all the help we can get haulin' water from a well outside of town. You volunteer for a trip and I'll see that you and your horse get watered."

"Much obliged," Slocum said, almost falling from the saddle. He collapsed into a chair in the shade along the west side of the store and tried to keep from gulping the water brought him by the storekeeper.

"Have I seen you somewhere before?"

Slocum looked up, wondering if he would have to shoot it out. The marshal was the only one in town who had gotten a good look at him the night before, but those in the crowd might have caught more than a glimpse of his face.

"Can't rightly say," Slocum said. "I just rode over from Nebraska. Biggest mistake I ever made."

"Not going to argue with you. We're losin' a dozen people a day from Cam—Dehydration," the man said.

"Was the town named Campbell? Thought I saw a sign with that name on it along the road."

"Was until the son of a bitch built a dam and cut us off from water in the Sulphur River. Keepin' it all for himself up there in the foothills. Said this town was his, so he could kill it if he wanted. And he wants to. His cattle are drinkin' their fill while humans are down here dyin' of thirst. Ain't right. Just ain't right."

Slocum said nothing. His run-in led him to believe the owner of the Circle C was capable of about anything. There hadn't been a single hint of gratitude for returning his son or burying the other man.

"You try buying water from him?"

The storekeeper snorted in contempt.

"We tried everything. We offered to buy the water, we offered to buy his spread. Then we tried to blow up that dam of his. Nothing worked."

Slocum remembered the alert sentries. A man of Campbell's choler would skin any guard alive who let someone near enough to destroy the dam.

The storekeeper made a funny little noise and then said in a voice almost too low to overhear, "Hell and damnation, we even tried to kill the son of a bitch."

"If Campbell founded the town, why'd he turn on it so quick?" Slocum asked.

"He thinks more of the Circle C than he does the town. That ranch of his was his wife's, and she upped and died a couple years back. Ole Trent Campbell ain't been right in the head since."

"What about the rest of his family?" Slocum hesitated to mention Marsh by name since that might get the man thinking about having seen him before.

"Folks have said he's savin' the Circle C for his son. Marsh ain't a bad sort, but he's Trent Campbell's spawn.

Right now, with Campbell actin' the way he is, that's enough to put the lot of them's necks in nooses. Or so say some people. Me, I'd settle for tarrin' and featherin', then drinkin' their water." The man coughed, then added defiantly, "I ought to say *our* water. Campbell don't have any more right to the water than anyone else, and no less, either. If he'd taken his share and left the rest from the Sulphur River for us in town, there wouldn't be this bad blood."

Slocum nodded. He had heard of less likely feuds. One that had raged down in Texas had started over a stolen pig and spare ribs. Fourteen men and three women had died over the span of eighteen months of traded accusations and bullets. If a small porker could cause such mayhem, stealing the life's blood of a town—its water—was likely to bring out even more potent feelings.

"What do you intend to do about it? You said folks were leaving Dehydration. Are you?"

"I like it here, leastwise most years. Can't imagine why the winters have been so mild and the summers so hot for the last couple years. When me and the missus first came to Campbell, the Sulphur River ran forty feet wide and a dozen feet deep. Not much if you come from back East like we did, but it was the elixir of life for this part of Wyoming."

"This can be a pretty part of Wyoming," Slocum said, remembering the endless prairie he had crossed to reach Dehydration. The promise of the Grand Tetons farther west drew him like a magnet, but it would take a day or two for him to recover enough to start for those purple-cloaked peaks. His eyes drifted out to his Appaloosa, judged his time estimate to be about right for the horse, too, then leaned back and sipped more at the water.

"That's one reason I took up the collection," the storekeeper said. "We have a five-thousand-dollar reward out for anyone who can get us water. We don't much care how they do it, either."

Slocum heard the edge returning to the store owner's voice, as if he was daring Slocum to use his Colt Navy to take down Trent Campbell. That wasn't going to happen.

"Don't have any ideas on that score," Slocum said, "but I'll be glad to work a day or two freighting water to pay you back." He held up the empty dipper. "Who do I report to for duty?"

"Reckon I'm the one," the man said, shoving out his hand to shake Slocum's. "Name's Pete Tahlmann and I'm about all the authority there is in Dehydration now. Became mayor by default since nobody else's dumb enough to want the job."

"What about the marshal?" Slocum asked, not wanting to tangle with the lawman. Without realizing he did so, Slocum rubbed the spot on his belly where the lawman had thrust his shotgun the night before.

Tahlmann laughed harshly and said, "He left town sometime in the night. We had a bit of disturbance last night—I missed out on it entirely—and it spooked ole Goat Butt."

"Goat Butt?"

"The marshal," Tahlmann said, laughing. "That's what I called him. Most of the people did, too. His name was Goble and was as worthless a marshal as any man you could find. He worked for Trent Campbell until he got fired when he lost a half-dozen calves to a pack of wolves, then the drought began to grip down real hard on us." Tahlmann shrugged. "We felt sorry for Goble, so we hired him. Wasn't much for him to do since we're a peaceable place."

"Not too many people left to break the law—or anyone who'd much care if they did," Slocum observed.

"You want the job?"

Slocum laughed harshly and shook his head.

"Didn't figure you would. If it comes down to haulin' water and havin' a blowhard throwin' his weight around, we need the water more."

"When do you want me to get to work?" asked Slocum.

"We got enough for a day or two. Rest up. You need it. Drink what you want but don't you dare spill a drop. As touchy as everyone is right now, that might get you lynched."

"Peaceable town," Slocum said.

Pete Tahlmann laughed uproariously.

"I'm takin' a real shine to you, Slocum. We need someone 'round here with a sense of humor since things are so grim, otherwise."

Tahlmann gave him another dipper of water and hurried off when he saw a potential customer walking through the front door of his store. Slocum sat in the shade and enjoyed his water, feeling life trickle back into his body slowly. From the way his Appaloosa noisily drank, Slocum knew he had to stop the horse or it would begin to bloat. He sucked down the last drop of water, got to his feet and dragged the Appaloosa away from where it had staked out a spot directly by the water barrel.

"Come on. I don't want you drinking so much that you explode," Slocum said, tugging hard to turn the horse's face and get it away from the water. "How about some food? Grain?" The horse stared at him, then tossed its head and tried to return to the water barrel for more. Slocum became insistent and pulled the horse away, leading it down the street to the livery stables. The Appaloosa finally relented and walked alongside Slocum until he secured it in a stall.

As Slocum returned to the main street through Dehydration, he heard loud cries and the snap of a whip. Curious, he followed the sounds to the edge of town where he saw a man dressed in a black cloth cutaway coat, gray-and-white–striped trousers and a tall silk stovepipe hat that would have looked more in place on a politician's head.

"Where's the high muck-a-muck in this fine town?" The

man whipped out a silk handkerchief and swiped at the rivers of sweat on his forehead. "I am none other than Conrad Ballantine, and I have come to relieve the drought in your bailiwick."

"Do we have a bally-wick?" asked a citizen of Dehydration. "Do we need one?"

"My good sir, what you have is heat. Too much oppressive heat and not enough gloriously damp moisture precipitating from the heavens above your heads!"

"You mean we ain't got any rain? I'll grant you that much."

Slocum moved closer and got a better look at the contents of Ballantine's wagon. Most of the crates were covered with a tattered brown tarpaulin, but here and there painted wood slates poked out where wind had blown away the canvas. Slocum wondered if all the crates Ballantine had actually contained explosives. A quick count of more than forty crates began to worry Slocum. If they were all filled with dynamite, Ballantine had more than enough to blow up the entire town.

He wondered if the man intended to blow Campbell's dam and release the trapped water from the Sulphur River. There was nothing said in the flyer about how the task of returning water to Dehydration had to be accomplished. Slocum realized there might be a horde of gunfighters descending on the town to start a range war. Conrad Ballantine might be the least of the lot.

"Allow me a few hours and I will have water cascading from the sky once more. I have petitioned the patent office of the great United States of America to protect my marvelous invention but, against the advice of my legion of able lawyers, I will reveal the details to you because of your great need."

"You got some sort of machine in that wagon?" asked someone in the crowd.

"I shun such mechanistic approaches. I am a chemist, I

am an aeronaut, I am a bringer of rain to the fine town of . . ." Ballantine looked around for help.

"They renamed it Dehydration," Slocum called out.

"I intend to be *the* bringer of rain to Dehydration," Ballantine finished grandly, striking a pose, left hand gripping the lapel of his fancy coat as he stared into the cloudless blue sky.

"How you reckon on doin' that?" asked someone else.

"It has long been known that explosives produce rain," Ballantine said.

"Yeah, a rain of rock and dust." A snicker went up through the audience.

"Placed high enough in the limitless sky, an explosion will shock the very drops of water from their hidden lodging and cause them to plunge to the ground! Rain! I will produce rain!"

"Call me when you get it fallin'," said someone at the back of the crowd.

"Call me ten minutes 'fore it rains," said another. "I want to strip off my clothes and run naked through it."

Laughter echoed from one end of Dehydration to the other as the people who had been curious about Ballantine now turned and went back to their business. It was too hot and too dry to stand in the sun waiting for a crackpot to blow up empty air.

The others left, but Slocum had nothing more interesting to occupy him. He walked closer and poked under the tarp, only to have Ballantine step down on one edge to keep him from looking.

"A magician never reveals his tricks, sir," Ballantine said.

"Is that all dynamite? You've got enough to blow up half of Wyoming."

"No, sir, it is not all dynamite. In fact, I have only those cases you saw. The rest is carefully packed equipment for lofting the explosives to the proper altitude to generate a significant rainstorm."

"You're sending dynamite up in a balloon?" Slocum

shook his head. He might have heard of more harebrained ideas in his time, but at the moment he couldn't remember what they might be.

"You are a man of great discernment, sir," Ballantine said. "Would you care to earn a few dollars aiding me? I require minimal crew, but as you can see, I am alone, my able assistants spread out across the state."

"Got arrested?" Slocum asked. From the shock on Ballantine's face he saw he had hit on the truth. A charlatan like Conrad Ballantine might have been run out of most towns, and not a few would have jailed his assistants because they weren't quick enough to catch him.

"I'm in need of a doughty assistant. You, sir, look as if you might fill the bill. Are you for hire?"

Slocum shrugged. He had nothing better to do until Pete Tahlmann sent him to fetch water for the town.

"Excellent, sir, you are now in the employ of Doctor Conrad Ballantine."

"Doctor?"

"A doctorate in philosophy, sir," Ballantine said pompously.

"You spend a lot of time thinking about thinking?"

Ballantine looked startled, then laughed.

"You are a man of infinite wit, sir. We shall get along well, as long as you do as you are told when you are told." Something in the way he said it put Slocum on guard.

"What do I have to do?"

"I need to assemble a balloon capable of lifting fully fifty pounds of dynamite into the skies where the explosion will stimulate the precipitation."

"The explosion'll make it rain?" Slocum found himself as skeptical as the men in the now-dispersed crowd.

"That it will. I have done extensive research into the matter and know it will work."

"Have you tried this before?"

"Grab hold of that tarp, sir, and pull out the equipment beneath it." Ballantine looked sharply at Slocum, as if daring him to pursue his line of questioning. The expression on Ballantine's face answered Slocum's question. This malarkey wasn't likely to hurt anyone, and it provided a diversion for Slocum.

"How much are you paying?" Slocum asked as he pulled out long, thin crates and placed them in order according to the numbers stenciled on the end panels.

"Why, uh, fifty cents a day."

Slocum looked up from his work, then laughed.

"Keep the money. I'll help for nothing." Slocum laughed a little harder and shook his head. "Hell, fifty cents *is* nothing."

"You have a strong work ethic, sir."

"My curiosity's stronger, and you know what they say about curiosity and cats." Slocum put his back to dragging out long strips of silk from the crates.

"Place the balloon panels side by side. Alternate colors, though it is not necessary. Just create an eye-catching pattern."

Slocum pulled the silken strips out to their full twenty-foot length and didn't pay a lot of attention to artistic creation. He saw how the strips laced together and, when Ballantine began weaving leather thongs up and down the strips to fasten them together, Slocum did likewise. Within an hour they had a large lump of silk spread out across the prairie.

Ballantine stepped back and looked at their handiwork. He smiled broadly, wiped sweat and then looked at the sky.

"No clouds to be seen," Slocum said.

"That's not my worry. I don't need clouds to precipitate rain. However, I should launch near sundown."

"Another hour or two," Slocum said. Getting closer to the eastern slope of the Grand Tetons accelerated sunset. "What's so important about sundown?"

"The air current aloft must be properly arrayed," Ballantine said. "That and it makes one hell of a fine fireworks show when it's set off at twilight."

Slocum found himself taking a liking to the pompous dandy. At Ballantine's direction, he stretched out the silken bag, then found wood and dried grass to build a fire in a deep pit.

"The hot air from the fire will rise into the bag, inflating it," Ballantine explained as Slocum worked to dig the pit deeper. "We won't be able to hold the balloon very long once it begins to rise. By then the crate of dynamite must be attached and ready to blow."

"You light the fuse, then release the balloon?"

"Exactly, sir. You are a quick study. Are you certain you have not done this before?"

"Saw a hot air balloon launched down in Louisiana once," Slocum allowed. "The owner of a whorehouse wanted to draw some attention to his establishment."

"I am sure he succeeded," Ballantine said, looking a trifle uneasy at such a use for a balloon.

"Surely did," Slocum said. "One of his ladies got her foot caught in a rope and was pulled aloft dangling upside down. She wasn't wearing any underwear."

"Uh, that will not happen this time. Our intent is to cause rain to fall."

"His intent was to advertise, and he succeeded in spades. Wasn't a man within ten miles who didn't hear the story and want to spend some time with that particular soiled dove."

"Your story is, uh, fascinating. Grab those lines and stake out the balloon so it won't go sailing off before proper scientific calculations are performed."

Slocum did as he was instructed but kept an eye on Ballantine as the man unloaded an entire crate of dynamite. He showed some familiarity with blasting caps and black miner's fuse, but Slocum still felt uneasy. It was as if Ballantine had read the proper way of attaching the blasting cap and fuse but had never actually done it.

"You ever do that before?" asked Slocum.

"It's all under control, sir. Fear nothing." Ballantine stood and stared at the spiderweb of black fuse as if it all confused him.

"How long'll it take the balloon to get up high enough for you?" asked Slocum. "From the fuse you've got on there, it'll explode in about a minute."

"A minute? Why, no, longer. I need it to rise for at least five minutes."

"Then put five feet of fuse on your cap," Slocum said. "It burns at a rate of one foot every minute. That's easy enough for most miners to figure out and keep from getting themselves blown up."

"Why, yes, of course. I knew that." Ballantine began replacing the short fuse with six and seven foot lengths. By the time he finished, it looked as if the crate of dynamite had grown spidery legs.

"You want me to round up a crowd?" asked Slocum. "Sun's just now slipping behind the mountains."

"Go on, get as many as you can. Especially the mayor."

"That'd be Pete Tahlmann."

"Yes, him, definitely. Get a lot of them, and I'll stoke the fire hotter." Ballantine began dropping dried bundles of grass around the heavier, thicker stacked firewood in the bottom of the fire pit. He struck a lucifer, dropped it and then recoiled as the intense fire exploded upward. "Excellent," Ballantine muttered. Slocum wondered if the man had any idea at all what he was doing, but he went off to gather the townspeople. So little happened in Dehydration, other than watching more of their neighbors and friends leaving town, this proved a needed diversion for most of them.

"You think the varmint has a ghost of a chance to cause rain, Slocum?" asked Pete Tahlmann.

"Can't say," Slocum allowed. "I don't understand what he thinks will happen, but it's sure to be pretty."

"You, sir, over here. Hurry, hurry. We must not waste another instant," called Ballantine. He waved imperiously to Slocum and pointed out the top of the balloon. "Lift it up. Let the hot air flow inward . . . and upward!"

Slocum did as he was told and was surprised at the sharp pull on the balloon as the heated air rushed into the silken bag. The bag inflated, expanded, took on an onion shape that Slocum had not suspected. Ballantine worked furiously to attach ropes to the bottom of the balloon.

"Walk it upright. Hang on to the side ropes. Keep it from launching. Some of you strong men, help him."

The balloon was held down by a half dozen men hanging onto the guide lines. This gave Slocum the chance to step away and watch Ballantine fasten the dynamite onto the balloon. The silken bag began straining at the leather thongs holding the panels together. Before Slocum could warn Ballantine, the man lit the miner's fuses dangling from the dynamite crate.

"Let her ascend to challenge the very gods of Olympus!" cried Ballantine.

"Drop the ropes," called Slocum. His command was obeyed, and the balloon surged upward. For a heart-stopping moment, Slocum thought the crate of dynamite would come loose and fall back to earth, maybe into the fire pit. But Ballantine had secured it well enough to sway to and fro beneath the opened mouth of the hot-air–filled balloon. It rose swiftly.

Slocum saw why the man had wanted to launch at sundown. The silk glowed for a few seconds until the air inside began to cool, but by then the balloon was caught on the wind and soared higher into the sky.

"What's supposed to happen?" asked Tahlmann.

"Rain, my good man, rain. I should have gotten out my

umbrella. We are all going to be drenched. You could make a fortune selling rain slickers."

"If we get rain, everyone'll want to be drenched," Tahlmann said.

Slocum watched as the balloon rose higher and higher into the air until it was several hundred feet above their heads. He tried to estimate how long before the dynamite went off, but he couldn't make out the dangling fuses in the darkness.

As he stared at the balloon, the dynamite went off with a roar that caused Slocum to stagger back from the concussion.

"Prepare for the rain!" cried Ballantine. "It's coming. Get ready for God-sent precipitation from heaven above!"

"Son of a bitch!" cried Tahlmann. "That's a burning cinder I got hit with. It's raining, all right, you ignoramus, it's raining wood from the crate you set on fire with all that dynamite."

Slocum saw that Tahlmann was right. Tiny fireflies fluttered from above, each sizzling and crackling. He was the first one to realize the small cinders would set fire to the dry grass all around. He shouted orders and sent the men running to get rakes and shovels to throw dirt on every smoldering patch.

Slocum went to Ballantine and took the man by the arm, steering him toward his wagon.

"You want some advice? Get in that wagon and drive out of here as fast as you can. They're likely to string you up if any of your hot cinders set fire to their town."

"I, uh, yes, you are so right, sir. Thank you. Thank you!"

Slocum saw Conrad Ballantine struggling to get his skittish team pulling, then went to help stomp out any burning patch of grass before it spread. It had been one hell of an interesting day. Slocum had to wonder what other cockamamie schemes would be tried to get water flowing back through the town of Dehydration.

3

"You got the look of a man who's been behind a team before," said Pete Tahlmann. "That so?"

Slocum nodded. He ran his hands over the reins and tugged a little to settle the four-horse team hitched to the heavy wagon.

"Been a while, but I'm good with horses."

"You got to be more than that. You've got to wrestle barrels of water into the wagon."

"Got the planks I asked for loaded?" Slocum glanced over his shoulder and saw the heavy wood planks resting in the wagon bed. "The rope, too?"

"Ever'thing you asked for, Slocum. And I even scared up two strong men to help you fill the water barrels and load them." Tahlmann put his fingers into his mouth and whistled shrilly. Two men lumbered out. Neither looked as if they had sense enough to come in out of the rain. It was a good thing there wasn't much chance for them to be faced with such a dilemma.

"Get into the back," Slocum said to the pair. To Tahlmann, he said, "If your map's good, I should be back with a full load of water sometime tomorrow afternoon."

"The map's good. You might have to shoo away all the

deer and rabbits from that watering hole. I suspect there's not many left in this area." Tahlmann turned and glared in the direction of the canyon Trent Campbell had dammed up.

Slocum snapped the reins and got the wagon lurching along. He drove past the spot in the road where Marsh Campbell and his partner had gone off the road, past the rock-covered grave and then farther out onto the prairie until he saw the deep ruts carved in the ground. Tahlmann hadn't joked when he said Slocum wasn't likely to miss the turnoff from the road.

"That's the spot," called one man in the rear of the wagon. "Me and Jimmy, we been out here before."

"How much farther?" called Slocum. He had it figured around ten miles, according to everything Tahlmann had said. The road was good and the team pulled well. He expected to reach the watering hole before twilight.

"Can't say," Jimmy called. "Me and Eddie, we're not so good at guessin' things like that."

Slocum settled down to drive, but perked up when he saw tracks leading away from the main ruts. He stood and craned his neck to see farther afield. Then he smiled. Slocum stomped on the brake as he pulled back hard on the reins to stop the wagon.

"You boys wait here. I've got some business to tend to."

"You goin' to take a leak?" asked one of them. Slocum had trouble separating Eddie from Jimmy. "Kin we take one, too?"

"I won't be five minutes," Slocum said. He pushed through the tall, dry grass and made his way along the new track pioneered by Conrad Ballantine's wagon. He found the man asleep in the shade beneath it. Slocum looked in the wagon bed and was surprised to find a couple cases of dynamite. The rest of the cargo—the balloon—was gone. But the explosion under the balloon had been so immense that Slocum reckoned Ballantine had used all the explosives he had.

"Who's there? I say, who's prowling about my camp?"

"It's me. John Slocum. You doing all right?"

"Oh, my erstwhile assistant. Yes, thank you, I am doing well. I need to regroup and consider different options."

"If you show your face around town, they're likely to regroup your body into different options," Slocum said, grinning. "What are you going to do now?"

"Win that five-thousand-dollar prize, of course. My theory is good. Explosives detonated in the air can produce a rainfall of significant portions," Ballantine said pompously. "Lacking an aerial delivery system now, I must find some new method of achieving my result."

"Blasting holes out on the prairie to see if water bubbles up might be the best use for that much dynamite," Slocum said.

"Is there water nearby?"

"The town's got a secret watering hole a few miles off. Wait until I roll back past tomorrow before checking it out," Slocum advised. "Otherwise, my two helpers might tell Tahlmann and anyone else who'd listen where you are."

"Much obliged, sir," Ballantine said. He tipped his tall hat in Slocum's direction and executed a bow as if facing a monarch of some foreign country. Slocum shook his head as he walked away. Conrad Ballantine was a weird duck, no doubt about it.

"Back in the wagon, men," Slocum called when he saw that Eddie and Jimmy were nowhere to be seen. It was too much to hope that they had wandered off and gotten irretrievably lost. Before he snapped the reins to get the team pulling again, he felt the thumps of their heavy bodies collapsing into the wagon bed. The drive to the watering hole went quickly and then the world collapsed around him.

Slocum stood in the driver's box and stared at the dry hole.

"Eddie, Jimmy, is this the right place?"

"Surely is," Eddie said, jumping to the ground. "Lookee

there. My pocket knife I lost last time I was here." He pried it loose from the dried mud and brushed it off before sticking it into his pocket.

"No question this is the town's water supply?"

"Nope, none. 'Cept there ain't no water here," said Jimmy. "What happened to it?"

"All dried up," Slocum said, climbing down and walking around the mud flats before kneeling. He poked about in the dried mud with a stick and found some evidence of water seeping up from below. But the artesian supply was gone, for whatever reason. He didn't know why water bubbled up in some places and not others—or why this should decide to vanish now.

"What're we gonna do? We got to take water back or Mr. Tahlmann'll be mighty sore at us," said Jimmy.

"Not your fault," Slocum said. "It's nobody's fault when a water hole dries up, especially in weather like this." He circled the area, wondering if it might have been fed by the Sulphur River. The best Slocum could figure, the river dipped below ground now and then went on its way from its headwater to wherever it finally petered out. With Campbell damming the river the way he had, it not only petered out fast but also caused watering holes like this one scattered around the countryside to eventually go dry, too.

"We might put some of the mud into the barrels," suggested Eddie. "We kin take 'em back 'nd let the sun dry out the mud."

"The water'd be gone but the dirt'd still be there, dummy," said his partner.

"But not if we—"

Slocum left the two arguing the best way to move mud back to Dehydration and get water out of it. He knew there was no point in that. Even if he had some way of separating water from dirt, there'd be scant amounts of water for anyone to drink. He had twenty barrels in the rear of his wagon, all needing to be filled for the town to survive another week. Slocum circled the area, then ranged farther afield, hoping the contrary water might have popped out of the ground somewhere else.

What he found didn't please him, but it was better than returning with empty barrels. Sticking his face up to the sky, he sniffed deeply and caught a heavy sulfur odor. Slocum turned slowly and homed in on the direction where the acrid scent was most intense. He walked steadily from the old watering hole across the prairie and not a mile off found another pool of water.

He knew what he had found before tasting the water. Tiny flowers of sulfur sprouted like living things at the edge of the water where evaporation had left behind a yellow powdery load. Cupping his hands, he brought the water to his lips, then spat it out. The sulfur content was so high it would choke a mule.

Slocum stood and looked at the pool he had discovered. It tasted awful, but it was water. Getting the sulfur from the liquid had to be easier than getting dirt out of mud. He just had no idea how to do it. Retracing his path to the dry watering hole, he called out to his two assistants.

"Get into the wagon. We've got work to do."

He drove the mile to the new pool and got Eddie and Jimmy to work unloading the barrels.

"We cain't drink this! It's got sulfur in it," protested Eddie.

"Then don't drink it. Just fill the barrels and load them into the wagon."

"If we cain't drink it, what good's it gonna do us?"

"I'd've thought a smart guy like you would have figured that out by now," Slocum said. Both Jimmy and Eddie screwed up their faces in concentration, working on the problem. Slocum hoped they'd share the answer with him if they came up with a solution. He didn't have the foggiest idea what good the sulfur-laden water would do anyone back in Dehydration, but the lure of so much potentially drinkable water might spur some genius.

As they worked, Slocum considered alternative ways of getting the water into the barrels without having to unload them, fill them with buckets, then roll them back up the two planks into the wagon bed. A hose and some way to pump the water would eliminate most of the work. Slocum wondered if Dehydration had a fire department with a pumping engine. There wouldn't be anything to pump in it now, but he could put the equipment to good use out here and save a considerable amount of backbreaking labor.

They finished loading twenty barrels of the sulfur-water an hour after sunset. A fitful breeze blew across the grasslands, evaporating the sweat that had soaked Slocum's clothing.

"Here's some food," Slocum said, digging through the bag holding their meager provisions. "There's not much here, but it'll keep your stomach from rubbing up against your backbone."

"Cain't we fix somethin' hot? Cook it?" asked Eddie.

"I don't want to start a fire in the middle of all this dry grass," Slocum said. "A range fire could burn for a hundred miles and not stop even then."

"He's right," Jimmy said. "Remember how mad Mr. Tahlmann was 'bout that fella what set off all the fireworks last night? We mighta burned down the town."

The two argued and talked and reminisced, leaving Slocum out of their conversation. That suited him fine. He needed time to consider where he was heading and how he would get there. Without water, he wasn't going anywhere. And if he could figure out how to supply water to the town on a regular basis without traveling a dozen miles across the prairie, he might claim that $5000 reward for himself. That much money would keep him in clover for a year or more.

"Turn in for the night, men," he said when he got tired of hearing them bickering. "Morning'll come too soon."

"Won't it come the same time it always does?" asked Eddie.

Slocum spread out his bedroll and tried not to listen to their endless discussion of when morning would come.

True to his prediction, morning came too soon. Slocum stretched his aching muscles and felt as if he hadn't slept a wink. He gnawed at a few biscuits that would have been rejected by a hungry cavalry trooper, swallowed them dry and looked longingly at the canteen dangling at the side of the wagon. This was all the potable water they had left. A few swallows.

"Get moving," Slocum called to his two assistants. "We've got a long, dry drive back to town." He checked the barrels while Eddie and Jimmy roused themselves and picked up with their bickering as if they hadn't bothered sleeping all night long. Slocum wished the barrels had water he could down without choking, but the sulfur was too potent for that. This watering hole must be fed by an underground volcanic vent, ruining the water.

"Why we takin' it all back if we cain't drink none of it?" asked Eddie.

"Tahlmann sent us for water, this is the best we can do. Might be he has some way of cleaning up the water."

"Oh, yeah, right. Mr. Tahlmann sent us." That satisfied the two men as they hunkered down in the rear of the wagon. Slocum climbed into the driver's box and got the team moving. The horses were mighty thirsty by now, but there was nothing he could do about it.

Slocum found himself drifting into a half-sleep as the wagon rattled along, returning to the main road to Dehydration. He snapped awake when he heard the neighing of another team.

"What's that?" called Jimmy, waking for the first time since they had left the sulfur hole that morning.

"It's a stagecoach," Slocum said. "How often does a stage come to Dehydration?"

"Not so often now," Eddie told him. "Cain't remember when the last time they came by. I sorta miss 'em, too."

Slocum drew rein and stood, shielding his eyes against the sun. He saw a dust cloud some distance away and coming toward them fast.

"Looks like Dehydration is getting a passenger or two," he said. "Maybe it's only mail."

"I like gettin' letters," Jimmy said.

"Nobody writes you," said Eddie.

"Don't matter. I cain't read, but I like gettin' 'em. Miss Martha used to read 'em to me."

Slocum let the two continue their endless reminiscences and jumped down when it became apparent the stagecoach was continuing along this road. He moved to the side to hail it, just to talk and find out what news there might be elsewhere in the countryside. To his surprise, the stagecoach stopped some distance away.

Slocum watched the driver jump to the ground and go to the passenger compartment, open the door and help a woman down. She brushed dust off her skirts. As far as Slocum could tell, this did nothing to clean off her clothing, but at this distance he couldn't even make out her face. Intrigued, he watched as the driver went around to the rear of the stage and pulled a trunk down. It crashed to the ground. The driver dragged it so the woman could sit on it beside the road.

Then the driver tipped his hat, climbed back up and snapped a long blacksnake whip to get his team pulling again—back along the road he had just travelled.

"What do you think 'bout that?" asked Eddie. "He done left her sittin' all by her lonesome out in the middle of nowhere."

"Let's go see if she needs a ride," Slocum said. "She'll certainly cook her head in this heat."

He swung the team around and rattled and clanked along the road toward the woman. She stood and waved in

his direction, then stopped and turned. She stared at something coming across the prairie that was hidden from
Slocum's view.

Slocum whipped the horses to their maximum speed
when he saw two masked men with guns drawn ride up to
the woman. She put her hands into the air.

"Hi-yaaaa!" shouted Slocum, getting the men's attention. One turned in the saddle and fired at him. The range
was too great for any accuracy but Slocum saw what had to
be done. The woman had been abandoned, for whatever
reason, and two road agents had come along to rob her—or
worse. That was the only thing that made any sense to
Slocum, and it didn't make a whole lot of sense.

He didn't care. He continued snapping the reins to urge
the team on, down a gradual hill and then up the incline to
where the men were trying to grab the woman and pull her
onto a horse behind the gunman not slinging lead in
Slocum's direction.

"Hang on," Slocum yelled to the men in the rear of the
wagon. The team strained mightily, pulling the water-laden
wagon up the slope. As the team reached the summit,
Slocum jumped, hit the ground hard and rolled. He came to
his feet, Colt Navy in his hand.

The one gunman continued to fire at him, but his aim
close-up wasn't any better than it had been when Slocum
was a hundred yards away. Slocum squeezed off a shot that
caused the man to recoil and almost fall from his horse.
The horse reared, pawed at the air and swung about, forcing its rider to fight to stay astraddle.

Slocum fired again, this time at the man trying to drag the
woman onto the horse behind him. The man's hat flopped
back, the bullet drilling a hole in the brim. A leather thong
held the hat around the man's neck, but the woman used this
to try to strangle him. She grabbed the hat and pulled, forcing him to twist and thrash about until she was thrown free.
She hit the ground and sat, staring up at her two kidnappers.

Slocum fired again. This was all it took to drive the two off at a gallop. Slocum hurried to where the woman sat in the dust, getting his first good look at her.

Long midnight-dark hair cascaded down her back as she tossed her head and turned fiery eyes of ebony at him.

"Are you all right?" Slocum asked.

"Help me to my feet and I'll check," she said. Slocum held out his hand. She took his with strong fingers and pulled herself erect and looked down.

"Looks as if everything's in exactly the right place," Slocum said, seeing her full figure and graceful beauty. She looked hard at him, then smiled.

"I'm glad you think so. I'm not so sure I'm not bruised." She rubbed her behind where she had landed so hard. She hastily added, "There's no need for you to examine my injuries."

"Too bad," Slocum said. Before she could reply, he asked, "Why'd the stage leave you out here in the middle of nowhere? We're a good ten miles from Dehydration."

"Dehydration?"

"Used to be named Campbell but times changed and the mood of the townsfolk changed, too. Dehydration is more accurate."

"Yes, of course it is. The drought. That's what brings me here."

"I beg your pardon?"

"The drought. I—" The woman cut off her explanation in midsentence. Slocum turned and saw three men arrayed behind him. He reached for his six-shooter, then froze. Two of the men had him covered with rifles. He and the woman would be dead in a heartbeat if he tried to outshoot men with levelled rifles.

"Seems you're going to be kidnapped, no matter what," Slocum said. "And I didn't even get your name."

"Madelaine Villareal," she said. "And I don't think these men intend to kidnap me."

"You ready, ma'am?" asked the middle rider, the one without a drawn weapon.

"I . . . yes, I am." She brushed past Slocum, her arm touching his for the briefest moment. It had not been accidental. She smiled, then went to the rider who pointed.

"We got a buckboard for you. We'll load your trunk."

"What's going on?" Slocum called. The two riflemen never swung their Winchesters from dead center on his chest.

"Nothing that concerns you, mister."

Slocum heard the buckboard rattle off down the road away from town. A driver beside Madelaine Villareal kept up a steady string of conversation, but she took a moment to lean out and wave to Slocum, as if telling him everything was fine. Then the two riflemen wheeled their horses around and trotted off behind the third man and the buckboard.

"We gonna go back to town?" called Eddie from the wagon. "I wanna see if the stage left any mail."

"You dummy," said Jimmy. "The stagecoach turned around and cut south, heading toward Big Piney. Ain't gonna leave mail in Dehydration when it went south."

Slocum shut out the pair's arguing, got back into the wagon and drove for Dehydration, thinking all the way back of Madelaine Villareal and the peculiar scene acted out on the Wyoming prairie.

4

"Don't know what good this water's gonna do us," complained Pete Tahlmann. "You can't drink it without pukin' your guts out." He jerked his thumb in the direction of Jimmy and Eddie, both sicker than dogs. "I let them drink some."

Slocum didn't think it was fair of Tahlmann to use the pair to experiment upon but said nothing about this. He had other concerns.

"The usual watering hole was dried up. It might be from the Sulphur River being dammed or it could be that whatever fed it from below is gone."

"Leaves Dehydration high and dry, so to speak," Tahlmann said, scratching himself as he spoke. "The only things not missing the water are the cooties. I swear I got enough nits to start my own flea circus. Never thought I'd say it, but a bath'd be mighty nice right now."

"The water," Slocum said. "It's got sulfur in it, but that shouldn't hurt your hide none."

"You might have something there, Slocum. They got those health spas where you can take the water outside Colorado City, south of Denver. Never saw the point of lounging around in hot water with sulfur in it, but might be this is our way to stay alive."

"By becoming a northern health spa?" Slocum laughed. "Bathers need to drink something, in addition to steaming out their poisons in hot sulfur water."

"Just a touch of sulfur might not be too bad," Tahlmann said, scratching himself more vigorously. "We could sell it as medicine."

Slocum watched Eddie and Jimmy being sick and knew the sulfur content in the water they had brought back was too high.

"What's out there on the prairie, farther out to the east?"

"Some ranches," Tahlmann said. "Why ask? Think they might have water and we don't? I sent a rider around to check right after Campbell cut off our river. The ranchers are in as bad a state as we are."

Slocum explained what had happened after the stagecoach let Madelaine Villareal off in the middle of the road.

"Yep, Eddie's right. The stage probably went on to Big Piney."

"That doesn't matter. Two masked men tried to kidnap the woman, then three more came up with a buckboard—four men, if you count the driver. She went with them and didn't seem too upset over it."

"Lot of ranches out there. The Circle C has the best pastureland up there in the mountains, especially using all our water, but the Bar None and the Curly K spread out over a couple thousand acres each. If I had to guess, the man leadin' those who took the woman sounds a lot like Chester Jacks, the Bar None ramrod. He's a hard case, he is, but never heard anything really bad about him."

"I ought to ride out and see if the lady's all right," Slocum said, thinking aloud.

"Your horse'd die halfway there," Tahlmann said. "No water, 'less you found some you're not tellin' about."

"No," Slocum said, "but she was almost kidnapped. Who were the first two men? The ones wearing masks?"

"Who knows? Wyoming's a wide-open place, lots of

rangeland and not many laws. With the drought settin' people apart the way it has, they might belong to about any of the ranchers."

"Like Trent Campbell?"

"Why'd you say that? You think he wanted to grab that little lady? Why?"

Slocum regretted having said anything about Campbell. The mere mention of the name in the town that used to be his namesake always provoked anger. Too much happened without explanations, and he was tiring of it.

"No good reason. Who'd know the stage was going to stop out on the prairie and just leave her like that? The driver ought to have his head examined since he didn't leave her with any water."

"Might have thought she wouldn't need it, not if she was met and escorted somewhere real fast."

"To the Bar None?" asked Slocum.

"Why not?"

Slocum considered the matter. He knew nothing of Madelaine Villareal, but it hardly sounded as if she was likely to be paying a social call to a down-in-the-mouth ranch in the middle of a prairie ready to burst into flame from drought. He perked up when he heard a wagon clattering into town. For a place in the throes of a major drought, Dehydration might as well have been the crossroads of the West.

"Who might that be?" Slocum asked.

Tahlmann craned his neck around and peered into the street, then shook his head.

"Another damn peddler, from the look of him."

"You're the ones who posted the reward for bringing water back to town," Slocum said. He saw that the peddler had already parked his wagon smack dab in the middle of the street and was working to lower the small stage at the rear of the wagon.

"A snake oil salesman, that's what he is," Tahlmann said with finality. "You goin' to listen to his pitch?"

"Why not? There's not a lot else to do in town."

"We could go to the saloon and get drunk. That's about the only drinkable liquid around here."

"I've tried the beer," Slocum said. It had been bitter to the point of making him want to drink the sulfur water instead. The whiskey had been more palatable, but the price charged was astronomical. At the moment, Slocum would pay that for a good drink of cool, fresh water and to hell with the alcohol.

"You got a point. Let's see what"—Pete Tahlmann peered nearsightedly at the wagon—"Perfesser Leonardo's selling."

They ambled over as the small, waspish man dressed in a gray morning coat finished setting up a small table on the stage. He fussed over proper arrangement of tiny bottles filled with a dark liquid. Only when everything was done to his approval did he step back, strike a pose and boom out in a bass voice that rumbled throughout Dehydration, "Come one, come all. Step right up, don't push, don't crowd. You are about to see the miracle of the ages. I, Professor Leonardo, late of the world famous Sorbonne University of higher learning, scion of renowned scientists, benefactor to the sheiks of far-off Araby, bring to you the answer to your problems."

"I'm mighty thirsty. Ain't 'nuff in one of them bottles to quench my thirst," spoke up a man at the front of the crowd.

Slocum nudged Tahlmann and whispered, "You ever see that galoot before? The one talking to the professor?"

"Nope, he's a newcomer." Tahlmann sucked his gums for a moment, then added, "Ain't any newcomers to Dehydration, not since you came to town, Slocum. That's gotta mean he's in cahoots with the perfesser."

Slocum and Tahlmann fell silent as the exchange between the man in the crowd and Professor Leonardo progressed to the point of the man calling the renowned scientist a fraud.

"A fraud? You dare impugn my reputation as a premier researcher? You dare call me a pettifogger, a mountebank, a quacksalver?"

"I guess I am, if I knew what any of that meant," the man said, getting a laugh. Slocum knew what would follow.

"I am no saltimbanque out to hoodwink you. You doubt my claim, sir?"

"I don't believe you're tellin' the truth, if that's what you're sayin'."

"Come up here on stage, my good man. Don't be shy. I won't bite." Professor Leonardo clacked his teeth together and grinned wolfishly. "Now, what part of my claim do you disbelieve?"

"A drop of that stuff is the same as drinkin' a quart o' water. That don't make no sense."

"I have travelled widely in Persia and learned the secrets of their mystics. How do you think a camel can cross vast desert distances without a drink of water?"

"I dunno."

"It's a secret known to the Bedouins, those masters of the Sahara Desert. And I have captured it in my Water Extract. A mere drop on the tip of the tongue will furnish the equivalent of quart of water."

"You sure 'bout this?" asked the man Slocum believed to be a shill for Professor Leonardo. "My mouth's mighty dry 'bout now."

"Ah, a skeptic. Open your mouth, thrust forth your tongue and allow me to place a drop—a single drop—of Professor Leonardo's Water Extract there."

The peddler made a big production of plucking a bottle from his display table, taking out the cork and then using a medicine dropper to place a dark bead on the man's tongue. Slocum almost laughed at the histrionics that resulted. The man hooted and hollered and danced around like a chicken with its head cut off. Then he threw back his head and howled like a wolf at the full moon.

"I do declare, that almost drowned me!" he exclaimed. "I never took a better drink in all my born days!"

"There you have it. A skeptic turned into a believer." Professor Leonardo looked around as if checking to see if a lawman moved through the crowd to arrest him for such a whopper.

"It's been nigh on forever since I drunk my fill. But one drop and I remember what it was like." The shill licked his lips, then wiped them on his sleeve.

"A boon to your water-deprived community," Professor Leonardo called. "Five dollars a bottle. A princely sum, yes, but worth a hundred times that. There are more drops than stars in the nighttime sky in every bottle."

"You tellin' us that stuff'll replace water?"

"It sounds like a miracle, my good man, and it is!" Professor Leonardo held out the bottle, tantalizing the local with it. "How long has it been since you've had a good, long, cool drink? This will replace your need for water for a week, a month!"

"Too bad the marshal's left town. Even Goat Butt could see this is a swindle." Tahlmann heaved a deep sigh. "You reckon I oughta do something, Slocum?"

From the stage mounted to the rear of the peddler's wagon, Professor Leonardo handed over the bottles as fast as he could grab them. His shill took the money and stuffed it in his pocket, nobody in the crowd noticing the sudden change in his status in their eagerness to get a water substitute.

"How long before you think the professor will leave town?"

"He won't be stayin' 'round to collect any five-thousand-dollar reward for bringin' water to town, that's for certain sure," Tahlmann said.

"He won't have to," Slocum said, mentally tallying what Professor Leonardo was raking in. "He'll have enough to more than get him to another town."

"Might be we should just slow him down," Tahlmann

suggested. "Give the folks time to find the Water Extract's not gonna do what they think."

Slocum pushed through the crowd and haggled with Professor Leonardo over buying a bottle. The longer he argued, the more nervous the peddler became.

"Move on, fellow, let others have their chance to purchase the elixir," the shill said. Slocum saw that Leonardo used him as a guard as well as a way to spark interest—and belief—in the potion.

"I want to hear some of the people of Dehydration tell me how well it works. There's plenty of elixir to go around," Slocum said, pointing to crates of the concoction. "And you've got all day to sell it."

"We have to move on soon. We are morally bound to get the fine Water Extract into the hands of as many people throughout Wyoming as we can, not just the citizens of, uh, Dehydration."

"How's that, Perfesser?" asked Tahlmann. "Did I hear you say *we* had to move on. You mean that's your assistant helpin' sell the bottles? The same fella that was in the crowd doubtin' how good it would work?"

"Time to move on, Lawrence," the professor said. "They obviously do not perceive how efficacious my Water Extract can be."

Slocum drew his six-gun and rested it on the edge of the stage.

"I think what Mr. Tahlmann means is that those who've bought your snake oil should try it. They might want their money back." Slocum's grip tightened on the six-shooter when Lawrence made a move for what might be a hideout pistol.

"Think that gunk plugs holes made by a bullet?" asked Tahlmann, seeing the small play unfolding. "You might take a bigger swig of it, if that's what it'll do."

Lawrence had gone pale under his suntan.

"We don't want trouble. We'll pack up and leave. You

the law hereabouts?" Professor Leonardo stared at Slocum, then at Tahlmann.

"Concerned citizens," Tahlmann said. "I'm as close as it comes to bein' mayor, too."

"Might be I was amiss not seeking you out and getting the proper licenses?" Professor Leonardo said. "That's how it works in most places."

"This tastes like shit!" someone cried, spitting out the drop of Water Extract he had put on his tongue. "This is a gyp!"

"Sounds like the citizens of Dehydration have spoken," Tahlmann said. "Let's you and me talk about givin' the money back to everyone, just so you two gents don't get invited to a necktie party." Tahlmann swung up onto the stage and took the two men aside, talking earnestly with them.

Slocum pulled the cork on a bottle and sniffed. His nose wrinkled from the intense odor that gagged him. He went to a water barrel and started to drink to clear the taste in his mouth and smell in his nostrils when he remembered the water barrels were little better.

In disgust, Slocum dropped the bottle of Water Extract into the barrel of sulfur water and turned away. The hissing and churning in the barrel stopped him dead in his tracks. He turned and watched the bubbles rise to the surface, burst and then leave behind a yellow scum on the surface. Several minutes passed before the agitation deep in the barrel stopped. Slocum reached out, scooped a handful of sulfur from the surface and wiped it off his hand, using the wall of the building for the task.

He dipped his hand into the barrel and sloshed around a little. The water felt different.

"Anybody got a dipper I can use?" Slocum called.

"There, on a hook, for all the good it'll do you," said the man who had complained about Professor Leonardo's Water Extract.

Slocum took the battered tin cup down, thrust it deep into the barrel and quickly withdrew it. He spilled a little of the water onto his hand. It shone crystal-bright in the sunlight. Sniffing at it failed to reveal the sulfur odor he had found before. Slocum took a tentative sip, then quickly downed the entire cup. He quickly repeated the action, his thirst sated after four cups.

He waited for his belly to convulse from the sulfur, but it didn't happen. Slocum went to where the professor and his assistant were hastily packing.

"What deal did you work out with them?"

"They returned the money, so now they're leaving town," said Tahlmann. "No reason to do more."

"Might be a good idea to find out how he makes that Water Extract," Slocum said.

"Why?" Tahlmann cocked his head to one side. "You know somethin' I don't?"

"Do it," Slocum said. "You won't regret it."

Tahlmann went back to accost Professor Leonardo and got into a heated argument with him. A few minutes later Tahlmann came back to the edge of the stage and called to Slocum.

"He claims he doesn't remember what went into this batch. Every one's different."

"Confiscate the whole batch. Every drop of it, then chase him out of town with a promise not to come back."

"What do you propose we do with a dozen gallons of that horse piss? I'd be afraid to dump it on the ground for fear it'd pizzen the whole damned place."

"Get Eddie and Jimmy to help unload it," Slocum said. Tahlmann shrugged and went back to his negotiations with the professor. When the two bulky men showed up, Eddie carrying a rope, the professor quickly agreed to Tahlmann's terms.

"There you go, lads," Professor Leonardo said. "Enjoy my fine potion." Over his shoulder he called, "Lawrence!

Get the team hitched up. We can find another, more accommodating community and show *them* how to make it rain!"

Eddie and Jimmy struggled to move the kegs of the darkish potion from the rear of the wagon. They had barely rolled them away when the peddler got his wagon rolling out of town in a cloud of dust.

"All right, Slocum, what's goin' on?" demanded Tahlmann.

Slocum pried off the lid of another sulfur-water barrel and dropped a bottle of the Water Extract into it. The bubbling and roiling produced a heavy layer of pure sulfur on the surface. Slocum was more careful skimming this off, like extracting churned cream. He tossed it to the ground, then plunged the cup into the once-tainted water and offered it to Tahlmann.

The storekeeper tentatively tasted it, then gulped fast. A smile split his face.

"Damnation, Slocum, it fixed up the water real good. You ought to get the reward!"

Slocum shook his head. They had plenty of Professor Leonardo's concoction, whatever it was, to purify this batch of sulfur water. They might even find that only a little of every bottle purified an entire barrel. But that solved only a short-term problem. It did nothing to break the drought and return water to the town.

Slocum looked at Tahlmann, and they both spoke at the same time.

"The professor!"

Slocum finished the thought for them both.

"He said he knew how to make it rain. Do you suppose he really knows?"

"We've got to find out—and we let him drive right on out of town!" cried Tahlmann. "Stop the varmint! Stop him! Stop the peddler man!"

5

"Twenty barrels of water and we still got gallons of his pizzen left," Tahlmann gloated. "I just wish we knew what the stuff was. It's kinda oily and has a burn to it like nitric acid's been tossed in."

"Like some barkeeps put in their whiskey drinks to give them a kick," Slocum said, half listening to the storekeeper. Pete Tahlmann had been going on and on about how good the water tasted after the sulfur had been skimmed off the top. Slocum looked past this minor victory to the bigger problem. Dehydration still needed water or it would vanish from the face of the earth. No way existed for the citizens of the town to survive indefinitely without a steady, reliable water supply. They could haul more water from the sulfur springs, but eventually the "Water Extract" taken from Professor Leonardo would run out—and so would their luck.

"Never cottoned much to a drink laced with nitric acid, though some folks say that's the only way to drink. Reminds 'em of their time on the Mississippi riverboats, I reckon," said Tahlmann, laughing at the notion that anyone in Dehydration had ever ridden in such a fine style. He stretched and looked downright cheerful.

"Took a bath?" asked Slocum. His nose wrinkled slightly. Tahlmann at least had the sense to bathe in the sulfur water, leaving the purified for drinking.

"That I did, Slocum, that I did. And it felt good. Don't go tellin' folks that. They think it's silly to bathe too often, and I took a bath not more 'n a month ago. But I washed my clothes, too. Reminded me of the time back 'fore the missus died." Tahlmann held out an arm to show off his handiwork. Slocum saw the diamond sparkle of sulfur crystals on the sleeve. The sulfur would wear off eventually, but right now it gave Tahlmann's clothing a special look—and smell.

Slocum considered what might be keeping him in Dehydration. He had solved their water problem, for a while. He could get enough water, give enough to his Appaloosa, to ride higher into the Grand Tetons and find a mountain lake that wasn't beset by drought. The grass at higher altitudes would be green and luxurious compared to the dry straw that passed for fodder on the drought-stricken prairie.

He could ride on and nobody would care a plugged nickel's worth. He had become friendly with a few of the townspeople, and he might even consider Pete Tahlmann a friend, but he had left friends behind before and would do it again. Why not now?

"He said he had a way of making rain," Slocum said.

"He might have been spoutin' nonsense. But he did sound like he had the way to relieve our drought so we could thumb our noses at Trent Campbell."

Slocum noted how Tahlmann always returned to blaming the owner of the Circle C for all their woes. He didn't much blame the storekeeper since it was mostly true and wondered if his reluctance to leave Dehydration was, in part, due to the way Campbell had treated him. Slocum had returned the man's son when Marsh Campbell might have died and all he got for his trouble were rifles aimed at him as they chased him off. They hadn't even been generous with their water, when they had an entire lake of it behind the fancy-ass dam built across the Sulphur River.

"The professor did sound as if he had a plan, but then so did Conrad Ballantine. To hear him tell it, his explosives would cause a flood to rival the one Noah rode out in the Ark."

"So, Slocum, you goin' after the perfesser to find what he was blatherin' on about? I can't give you much money, but a few hundred dollars might grease the peddler's tongue."

"I'm not sure he'd be willing to tell me anything after we stole his Water Extract and threatened to stretch his neck if he didn't leave in a hurry."

"You underestimate yourself, Slocum. You're a persuasive gent, you are. Ride after him, find him and palaver a spell. It'll be up to you to decide if he has a good idea worth five thousand dollars."

"That'd be more than enough a lure to get Professor Leonardo to return."

"He didn't seem to know we had such a big reward out for anyone getting us water. The spiel he gave about his concoction was pretty standard fare, I'd say. He might have told the same story in a dozen different Wyoming towns and sold the same damn whangdoodle."

"I'll track him down and find out what he had in mind." Slocum considered seeing if Conrad Ballantine still camped out on the prairie. He hadn't been able to warn the balloonist that the water hole had gone dry and that the sulfur pond wasn't likely to do him much good. He vowed to take a couple bottles of Professor Leonardo's Water Extract to use as a peace offering.

"You got more 'n that on your mind, less I miss a guess," Tahlmann said. "That woman was a looker, wasn't she? Did you get her name?"

"She was mighty easy on the eyes," Slocum agreed.

"Might be your hunt for the peddler will take you to the Bar None ranch. Give my regards to 'em all and tell Chester Jacks that he's run up a mighty big bill at the store and I'd like a few dollars payment."

"Why ask the ramrod of an outfit for the money? Why not the owner?" Slocum saw there was something more to the story.

"If old Chet had bought anything, I would. Truth is, I'm just a better poker player."

"Or maybe he's just a lousy player," Slocum said.

"I shouldn't try bluffin' you, Slocum. You're a sight better player 'n me."

"Quit trying to bamboozle me." Slocum had the feeling Tahlmann was a fine poker player.

Tahlmann laughed, fetched a hundred dollars while Slocum pocketed a few bottles of the Water Extract, made sure his horse had drunk its fill, then headed after Professor Leonardo.

If he hadn't taken Tahlmann's money and ultimately the town of Dehydration's money, he would have given up and headed for the high country. Even with a full canteen and his horse properly watered for the first time in a week, the heat sucked moisture from his body and threatened to leave him as dried out as an old corn husk. Slocum pulled his hat down to shade his eyes and pulled up his bandanna to keep the dust from choking him as he rode. When he had left town he thought finding Professor Leonardo would be simple. How fast could the snake oil peddler travel in that battered old wagon of his?

Slocum found the answer. Leonardo travelled as if he had a feisty, well-rested quarter horse under him. Finding wheel ruts in the dust was impossible. The small breeze that blew fitfully across the prairie shuffled everything around just enough to erase tracks. An entire detachment of cavalry could have ridden this road a few hours earlier and Slocum wouldn't have found their hoofprints. So he rode. Steadily all day long, and still he hadn't found the peddler.

He began wondering if Leonardo actually had a way of making rain or if he had been shooting off his mouth. The Water Extract worked, but not in the way the self-styled professor ballyhooed. But what secret plan did the peddler have to cause it to rain?

Slocum wondered if he would find it funny if Professor Leonardo's idea was to float explosives aloft in a balloon. He didn't think so. As he topped a small rise, he caught the scent of meat cooking. Slocum stood in the stirrups and turned slowly, homing in on the fragrant odor that made his mouth water. He turned his Appaloosa off the road and headed in the direction of the cook fire. Slocum almost rode past before he saw the fire itself, dug far down into the ground.

"Evening, Professor," Slocum called. Professor Leonardo jumped to his feet, dropping the small tidbit of cooked rabbit he had been eating.

"What do you want? There's no way I'm going back to that godforsaken hellhole."

"Whoa, rein back," Slocum said. "Nobody wants you back there. I'm here on my own." Slocum looked around, wondering where the professor's assistant lurked. Lawrence was a bulky sort, more fat than muscle, but not to be underestimated. A man with a six-gun could shoot anyone in the back, given the chance.

"Why? You got all my Water Extract."

"What happened to your shill?"

"Lawrence lit out," Leonardo said sullenly. "We been a team for a year and he up and leaves, just like that." He snapped his fingers. The sound failed because of the grease on his fingers, but it didn't stop Leonardo from making his point. "No gratitude, none at all. We were partners."

Slocum heard more than the actual words the peddler

uttered. Lawrence had cleaned out any stake they might have accumulated before heading out on his own. Slocum fought down a smile. This was the perfect time for him to make his offer.

"As you were leaving town, you said there was a way of making it rain. Such information might be worth a few dollars."

"How many?" Leonardo suddenly gave his full attention to Slocum. His dark, hard eyes turned more ratlike by the instant.

"Fifty," Slocum said. "If I think the scheme might work."

"This is surefire. I've seen it done a dozen times. Never fails," Professor Leonardo said, rubbing his greasy hands on his pants. "A hundred."

"Seventy-five," Slocum said, knowing he still had a few dollars to offer if the peddler wanted to haggle some more.

"I tell you, you find the man who can bring the rain?"

"You're not able to do it yourself?" Slocum stared at Leonardo when the man laughed.

"This requires special talents, ones I don't have."

"Deal," Slocum said, wondering if he was being snookered. He got out the money and began counting off the bills, keeping the full size of the poke hidden from Professor Leonardo until he had the proper amount. He held it up, just out of the man's reach. "Who can make it rain?"

"I was up north of here, not more 'n a day or two travel and came across a band of Northern Arapaho. Their medicine man was telling about doing a rain dance to break the drought. But he needed things they couldn't provide, so he hadn't done it. But you find Elk Heart and get him whatever he needs and he'll have it pourin' for a week. Longer."

"A rain dance," mused Slocum. He wasn't sure if he believed the Northern Arapaho or any Indian tribe had the powers their medicine men claimed, but it wasn't any worse an idea than setting off dynamite a hundred feet in the air. And he had heard stories, especially from old mountain men, of the ritual dances and how well they worked.

He handed the money to Professor Leonardo, who grabbed it and counted it again before stuffing the greenbacks into his pocket.

"The Northern Arapaho were camped by Signal Peak, about twenty-five miles north of here. But that was three, four days ago, so they might have moved on. But if anybody can bring down the rain, it's Elk Heart. He's supposed to be the best medicine man in the whole damn tribe."

"Where are you heading?" Slocum asked.

"Big Piney. I want to get south to a town where they might have some water to spare."

Slocum bade Professor Leonardo good-bye, got onto his Appaloosa and turned northward, traveling back to the main road before deciding to bed down for the night. He stretched out and stared at the cloudless sky and the bright stars above him. The notion that the Northern Arapaho might break the back of the drought rolled over and over in his head until finally he slipped off to sleep.

The Northern Arapaho band made no effort hide their trail, making it easy for Slocum to find them within the week. He approached their camp slowly, to give them plenty of time to get used to the idea that they were getting a peaceful visitor. Even then, Slocum drew rein about ten yards away and sat silently, waiting for acknowledgment. He took the time to study the dozen braves in the band and determine who the leaders were. By the time the one he had pegged as the hunting chief came out, he knew who their medicine man was and had formed a few ideas to persuade the Northern Arapaho to come with him back to Dehydration for a formal rain dance.

"You are not a hunter," the chief said.

"I seek Elk Heart, a famous medicine man among your people and mine," Slocum said. He was as blunt as the chief, which was considered the height of rudeness. To reach this point should have taken the better part of a day sitting around a campfire, smoking a pipe and swapping compliments. Slocum thought it was the drought that made the Northern Arapaho chief so testy. It certainly had taken its toll on him. Finding more than a pair of watering holes that didn't spew forth sulfur-stinking water had been quite a chore. As it was, he sorely desired to partake of the sweet water in the hole not a hundred feet away from the Northern Arapaho camp.

He had been brusque and rude, but Slocum knew better than to simply help himself to the water. The Northern Arapaho might not have a deed to this land, to this water, but they considered it theirs. Since they outnumbered him twelve-to-one, he wasn't going to argue the point.

"You know Elk Heart?"

"He is famed for his rain dance. I would talk to him about doing a rain dance so both our peoples can benefit." Slocum took off his hat and brushed it across his leg. A cloud of thick brown dust filled the air to emphasize his point.

The chief made a quick hand gesture for Slocum to dismount and join them. Slocum hastily obeyed, leading his Appaloosa to a place where he could secure the reins to a rock outcropping. Only then did he join the Indians.

"He is Elk Heart," the hunting chief said, indicating an old man sitting with a blanket around his shoulders. Slocum had reckoned this was the medicine man since he was too old to be on a hunt. That meant this band of Northern Arapaho weren't hunting for meat but something else. If they had a medicine man with them, he had to approve whatever they found for the magic it contained.

Slocum didn't look directly at the old man; that would have been unconscionably rude, but he did nod slightly to show he understood how important Elk Heart was.

The chief motioned for Slocum to sit. For the next hour they passed around a cup of water, constantly filled by a young brave who dashed off to the watering hole when necessary, and talked of nothing much. Slocum chaffed at the delay but knew things were settling into a familiar, polite pattern now. When Elk Heart finally spoke, Slocum knew he had a good chance of convincing the Northern Arapaho to allow the rain dance back at Dehydration.

"There are many medicines I lack," Elk Heart said. "We have not found them. Do you have them?"

"There are many medicines in the town," Slocum said. "Everyone there will seek what you need."

"Juniper berries," Elk Heart said. "Also chokeberries. Whitebark from the pine. Squirrel fur taken from black bear scat. Bear grease. Other things, sacred things like tule powder."

"We'll find what you haven't already rustled up," Slocum assured him. "There are a hundred people in the town of Dehydration anxious for rain. They'll look for what you need until they drop from exhaustion."

"I do not know this Dehydration," Elk Heart said.

"It used to be called Campbell. It's just east of the Circle C ranch owned by Trent Campbell." Slocum held his breath when the hunt chief and Elk Heart exchanged looks. This might be a deal killer if Campbell had aggressively chased off Arapaho parties from his land—and his water.

"We know of this place."

"Campbell is not the one asking for the rain dance," Slocum added. He hoped he didn't sound too desperate. "He wants nothing to do with the town that used to have his name."

The chief nodded. So did Elk Heart. They sat in silent thought for almost fifteen minutes, letting Slocum stew. Then, when he worried that they would refuse the offer, the chief spoke.

"Our medicine man will accompany you to do this dance."

Slocum held his breath, waiting for the other shoe to drop.

"You will give him all the sacred items he needs." The chief sucked at his lower lip for a moment, then added, "You will give him twenty horses and a rifle, too."

Slocum considered haggling as he had with Professor Leonardo, then decided it wasn't worth it. Giving an Indian, and one probably off the reservation illegally, a rifle was a federal crime, but letting most of Wyoming suffer such a crushing drought was an even greater crime.

"Done," Slocum said.

"Done," Elk Heart echoed.

Slocum wondered what he had gotten himself into, then decided it hardly mattered. Either the Arapaho medicine man succeeded and provided the rainwater everyone wanted or he failed, leaving them no worse off than they were before.

6

Slocum rode back directly to Dehydration, letting the Arapaho band follow at a slower pace. He saw that Elk Heart wasn't able to ride long, arthritis taking its toll on the old medicine man. This worried Slocum a mite since Elk Heart had to perform the rain dance, but that was somewhere off in the future. Slocum had a list of items the medicine man needed for the ceremony, and some of it would be hard to come by. With the drought, the juniper hadn't put out many berries this year, and Slocum wasn't sure he had seen a single whitebark pine during his ride through Wyoming. These were the items best left to the locals to find.

"Hey, Slocum," called Pete Tahlmann, seeing him dismounting in front of the saloon. "You back so soon?" There was more than a hint of sarcasm in the storekeeper's words.

"What's wrong? Didn't you think I'd be back at all?" Slocum fumbled in his shirt pocket and pulled out the $25 he had left from the hundred Tahlmann had given him to barter with Professor Leonardo. "Here's what's left, but you're going to have to ante up twenty horses."

"You been dealin' with them damn redskins?"

"That was Professor Leonardo's suggestion. An Arapaho rain dance. I found a band of Northerns about where he'd said, so I reckon he knew what he was talking about. Their medicine man was already hunting for the sacred ingredients for a dance but hadn't found everything yet."

Slocum handed over the list he had scrawled on a scrap of paper stuffed into his pocket. Tahlmann held it up to the light and peered hard at it.

"You want us to scare up this shit?"

"Bear shit, with squirrel fur in it. Elk Heart specified black bear but grizzly might do."

"Grizzly bear shit, eh?" Tahlmann shook his head. "How we supposed to tell the difference between it and black bear shit?"

"That ought to be easy," Slocum said, flopping into a chair in the shade. "You folks know to wear bells to scare off the grizzlies, don't you?"

"Well, sure," Tahlmann said reluctantly.

"And you carry pepper, just in case the grizzly gets too close, so you can fling it into his eyes?"

"Everyone does," Tahlmann said.

"Then all you need to do is look for bear scat that doesn't smell like pepper or have bells in it."

Tahlmann hesitated a moment, then laughed ruefully.

"I was dead wrong, Slocum. I *don't* want to play poker with you. You'd skin me out of every nickel in my pocket."

"The band of Arapaho ought to be here in a day or two. They were travelling a considerable bit slower, but I wanted everyone hunting for what Elk Heart needed so it'd be ready when they arrived."

"Twenty horses? That's a mighty steep price."

"Cheaper than five thousand dollars," Slocum said. "Considering the swayback nags I've seen in this town, they wouldn't fetch more than twenty-five dollars apiece if you tried to sell them to a blind man. That makes Elk Heart's dance a bargain."

"If it works."

"If it doesn't, you don't have to give him the horses. There are only a dozen braves in the band."

"You workin' fer them or us?"

"If he gets it to rain, the answer's obvious. Both of you."

"No sir, I don't want to play poker with you or ever let you come callin', trying to sell me things for the store. With that silver tongue of yours, I'd buy supplies I wouldn't need."

"And you'd pay too much for them," Slocum finished. "Right now, I need a shot of whiskey to wash the trail dust out of my mouth. Buy me a drink?"

"Would like to," Tahlmann said, "but I've got a shopping list to fill. I'll get Eddie and Jimmy hunting for the squirrel fur in the bear flop. The berries I can get from the Widder Jenkins. 'Bout time I paid her a visit, anyway." Tahlmann smiled at the thought and sauntered off.

Slocum went into the bar and saw he was in time for lunch. He had a dry beef sandwich, just a slab of meat between two slices of bread, and washed it down with three bitter beers, then paid double what he had for the beers to get a tin cup of water to chase everything down. The water tasted best of all.

As he leaned back and relaxed, Slocum considered spending more of his money on a shot or two of whiskey. Before he came to a decision, he sat bolt upright in the chair and stared at the swinging doors leading into the main street. Slocum rubbed his eyes, thinking dust had blurred his vision. Or maybe the water had affected him like strong liquor.

"Come on back when you want another shot or two of water," the barkeep called as Slocum hurried to the entrance of the bar. Slocum ignored the man, pushed through the doors and stepped onto the boardwalk. He shielded his eyes against the glare to make certain his eyes weren't deceiving him. They weren't.

"Miss Villareal!" he called. The woman stopped, turned

and faced him. Slocum's heart almost missed a beat. She was even more beautiful than when he had seen her the first time out on the prairie. Her long dark hair had been put up in a fetching coiffure, and she wore clothing that hadn't been turned brown with dust.

"Why, Mr. Slocum. I was just thinking about you." Her bright, white smile rivalled the sun's radiance, and her ebon-dark eyes fixed boldly on his emerald ones.

"You don't have a gun in your hand, so I trust they were nice thoughts."

"Why ever would I want to shoot my savior? You didn't have to come to my rescue."

"Who were the men trying to kidnap you? Did you ever find out?" He saw her stiffen and her jaw firm, as if she clenched her teeth.

"I have my suspicions, but no proof."

"The others, the ones led by Chester Jacks, treated you well?"

"I am impressed, sir," she said. "You pursued the matter enough to find out who the men were?"

"He's ramrod for the Bar None. Did you have business there?"

"I spent some time in discussion there, yes," she said, "but I am more intrigued why you bothered to come to my aid in the first place."

Slocum's eyes never left hers. A little smile danced on his lips, and she eventually averted her eyes and might have blushed. It was difficult to tell because of her complexion, but Slocum thought she did.

Her eyes returned to his.

"I suppose the original attraction was mutual, but you did more than try to save a poor, lonely—"

"Lovely," he cut in.

"—woman from what seemed a predicament of her own making. Then you risked life and limb to shoot it out. *Then*," she went on before he could respond, "you inquired after me to be certain I had not come to some even greater harm. I am indebted to you and your sense of honor."

"Comes from my Georgia upbringing," he said.

"I thought I detected a hint of Southern accent," she said. "There is so much I don't know about you."

"And there's a considerable amount I'd like to know about you," Slocum finished easily. "My guess is that you're from New Mexico. Rich family, possibly original Spanish land grant owners—" Slocum stopped when he saw the expression on her face. "I'm sorry. I didn't mean to intrude."

"You have been prying, sir."

"Call me John." This took her aback. She had expected an apology.

"Very well, John. And you may call me Maddy."

"Madelaine Villareal. Maddy." The names flowed from his lips and floated on the air.

"You were guessing about that? My background?"

Slocum nodded.

"You are more observant than I thought. I underestimated you, and that is something I seldom do. Hmm," she said, as if considering some weighty matter. "You might be the perfect one to aid me again."

"What can I do?"

"I am looking for a boarding house where I might spend a week or so. Although a newcomer to the town, you seem to know it and its residents well."

"You're not guessing that I'm a newcomer, are you? Did you ask after me?"

Maddy opened her mouth to answer, then clamped it shut.

"I have my ways," she said. But Slocum found himself more intrigued than ever. She hadn't asked about him and yet she knew he was not a resident of longstanding in De-hydration.

"We might ask at the Widow Jenkins," he said.

"Of course, why didn't I—" Maddy stopped, smiled and extended her arm for him to take. "Will you escort me to Mrs. Jenkins's house?"

"I don't rightly know where it is. You're right about me recently coming to Dehydration."

"It's the two-story house at the north end of town."

"How long have you been gone from Dehydration?" asked Slocum. He knew by the way she drew away slightly from him that he had asked another question she did not want to answer. Holding back the obvious question of why she had returned was hard, but Slocum did so. He would never find out anything about the lovely woman if he kept asking questions that nettled her.

Oh, look, there's Mrs. Jenkins now," Maddy said, seeing the woman driving a buggy around to the front of the house.

"And Pete Tahlmann looks as if he's going somewhere with her. A picnic?"

"Yes, of course, a delightful picnic," Maddy said, as if laughing at a secret joke. Slocum saw from the way Tahlmann and the widow sat side by side in the buggy that they were going to enjoy more than deviled eggs and pickles at their picnic. It was obviously an open secret, and one dating back to whenever Maddy had been in Dehydration before.

"Lookee there," Tahlmann said. "If it isn't the señorita. Let me guess. Slocum was your knight in shining armor. I should have known, but he never told me your name. But I should have guessed."

"What can I do for you, Maddy?" called Mrs. Jenkins. "A room?"

"That would be wonderful, if you have one to rent."

"For you, of course I do. Go on in and find one that suits you. The one looking west, well, you might want to rent the one on the east. Settle in and we can talk about it later." The woman looked at Tahlmann, grinned like the cat who had

eaten a canary, then rocked back as he snapped the reins
and got the horse pulling the buggy. Tahlmann touched the
brim of his hat to Maddy as they rolled past, but he winked
broadly at Slocum.

Slocum had the feeling of being dropped into some
elaborate stage play where he was the only one who hadn't
read the script. They all knew one another, and Maddy was
reluctant to tell why. He would have to ask Tahlmann when
he returned from his tryst with the Widow Jenkins.

"Folks in this town surely are friendly," Slocum said.
"Trusting, too. Just go on in and find yourself a room. Poke
about while she's off with the storekeeper."

"Yes, it's a nice town," Maddy said, going up the walk
and entering the front door with a few panes of etched
glass mounted in it. Inside the house proved as elegant and
well-appointed as the door suggested.

"Nice place," Slocum said, looking around.

"Let's go upstairs and see the room," Maddy said, going
up the stairs with an easy grace that had Slocum watching
her the entire way. He followed and immediately looked
into the room facing west. It was large, airy and had a good
view of the Grand Tetons in the distance. Maddy was already in the room across the hallway looking over the
brown, desolate, drought-wracked prairie.

Slocum looked into the east-facing room and saw how
small it was in comparison. Worse, the room was like a
furnace since the sun shone directly on the window; not
even chintz curtains held back the heat.

"If the rooms rent for the same price, the other one's
larger and nicer," Slocum said.

"No." The woman's answer was sharp, curt and brooked
no argument.

"I'll help you with your things," Slocum offered. She
must have left her trunk somewhere in town, and getting it
to the house and up the stairs would be a chore.

"I'd hoped you would say that," Maddy said in a barely

audible voice. She moved closer and put her arms around his neck, then kissed him.

It took Slocum by surprise, but he recovered quickly. He returned the kiss with as much passion as she had shown. He might have gotten the wrong idea about the first kiss, but there was no mistaking the second. She broke off, chest rising and falling quickly now. She stared into his eyes and then turned abruptly.

"You said you'd help me with my things. Do it! Undress me!"

Maddy tossed her hair and got the long mane out of the way so he could unlace her dress. The garment seemed to pop off her body. He wondered how she had gotten into it and then he forgot about anything but the warm feel of her naked breasts as she turned and pressed against him again.

"It's mighty hot in here," she said. "Let me help you." Her fingers worked down his shirt, got off his gun belt, fumbled at the buttons on his jeans.

As she worked to get him stripped of his pants, Slocum's fingers explored the half-naked woman's body. He stroked over silken brown skin, down her arms, across her back, outlining each and every bone in her spine. His touch made her tremble and shiver a little in spite of the heat in the room. Both were sweating and shivering with anticipation by the time she worked his pants down and let his manhood come bounding out.

"So nice, so big," she said, dropping to her knees in front of him. She rubbed her cheek against his hardness, then lightly kissed the tip. Slocum felt an earthquake pass through his body that caused his knees to go weak. He had to prop himself up against the door when she took him in her mouth and began teasing him with feather-light touches of her tongue.

"When I said I'd help you with your things, I didn't know you meant you'd help me with mine, too," Slocum said. Sweat poured down his body, tickling as it dripped to the hardwood floor. He ran his fingers through her long black hair and guided her in a motion that sent his pulse racing even faster. When he thought he could no longer hold back, he moved her face away.

"No more?" she asked, her eyes dancing with arousal.

"More, but not that way," he said. He lifted her to her feet and then began caressing and kissing. He started with her lips and cheeks and closed eyes and throat. Then he worked down and popped each of the berry-firm nipples into his mouth for a little suckling and tonguing before moving lower. Her skirts were still fastened. It took both of them to free the unwanted garment and let it fall to the floor.

They clung to one another as if their lives depended on it, kissing and stroking, moving slowly to the silent music only they shared.

Slocum wasn't sure how they did it, but they spun around and somehow left the room, going to the larger one across the hall. He thought Maddy might hesitate because she had been so adamant against renting this room. If anything, her fervor increased.

She reached down and gripped him firmly, her hand almost throttling the life from him. He reached behind her and gripped a double handful of rump and lifted. Her legs parted gracefully and snaked around his waist so he supported them both. She wiggled her hips and used her grip to position him properly.

Then they both gasped as Slocum sank all the way to the hilt in her tight, moist tunnel.

Slocum's legs went rubbery and he leaned back against the wall, still supporting them both. The sultry woman's ankles were locked firmly behind his back, holding herself in position. When he got his balance by widening his stance a little, he lifted using the grip on her hindquarters, then simply released her. She rose and then sank back along his shaft. With a twitch of his hips and increasing co-

operation from the woman, they began bouncing and bob-
bing around, her hips rising off his rigid rod and then grav-
ity pulling her back down. She bounced and ground her
hips harder and faster.

Slocum held on for dear life and experienced the delectable feel of a woman's body entirely surrounding him.

The heat and pressure around his hidden length increased. Maddy began gasping for breath as she continued
to rise and fall. She tossed her head like a frisky filly to get
her long dark hair from her face. Slocum saw the mask of
utter desire etched there and bent low to kiss her breasts.
This forced the woman to lean back and jam her hips down
even more powerfully into his groin.

Slocum's world spun about in wild gyrations as Maddy
lifted her hips and tried to touch the floor by leaning completely backwards. He held her firmly and brought her into
his crotch even more powerfully. Their thrusting motion
turned into more of a circular one, and Slocum knew he
could no longer hold back. The fierce tides rising within
his loins were not to be denied.

He groaned even more when he felt the intense crushing
pressure all around his buried shaft. Maddy shivered and
shook as a flush rose to her cheeks, neck and breasts. The
carnal heat, the feel of the woman's female sheath tensing
about him, triggered Slocum's release. He blasted forth
into her yearning cavity.

They wiggled a few more times and then wobbled.
Slocum was too drained to support both their weights any
longer. He turned and sat heavily on the edge of the bed,
Maddy's legs still around his waist. She relaxed her grip and
kissed him, then looked past him out the window to the west.

"So there, you son of a bitch," she whispered.

Slocum recoiled. Maddy slipped away, still facing him,
and smiled.

"What'd you say?" he asked, wondering if the hammer-
ing pulse in his ears had masked her real words.

"It was sensational, John," she said. "So much fun, I want more." She dropped to her knees on the floor beside the large bed and gently parted his legs. "Oh, so tired looking. I know how to perk it up right away." She dived down like an eagle on its prey and took him into her mouth. In spite of their recent lovemaking, Slocum felt tingles and twitches as life returned to his organ.

Her eager, knowing mouth did all the right things—but Slocum had heard her bitter comment clearly.

"Umm, tasty," she said. Then Maddy rocked back and looked up at him. "What's that?"

"I don't know," he said. He heard the ruckus outside now, too. "Should we go look?"

"I don't know," Maddy said. "It won't be anywhere near as much fun as what we're doing."

Gunshots convinced Slocum to go into the room Maddy had claimed as hers and look out the window. A score of men with rifles lined the street, all pointing their weapons at a small band of Indians.

"Looks like Elk Heart got here faster than I thought," Slocum said.

"Indians?"

Slocum would have laughed, seeing her buck naked and staring out the window, if her outcry hadn't been born of real fear.

"Don't worry. It'll be fine," he said, climbing into his clothes. He hoped he wasn't lying to her. More gunshots told him Elk Heart's arrival wasn't being accepted too well.

7

"Put down the rifles, put them down now!" Slocum shouted above the hubbub of the crowd. "They aren't attacking. I asked them here. They're going to bring rain."

"What? How's them savages gonna bring us water? You mean we're gonna let them haul water fer us from the sulfur hole?" asked a weathered old man who looked more like a prospector than a merchant.

"Quiet down! Pete Tahlmann will explain everything," Slocum shorted, hoping Tahlmann and Mrs. Jenkins would end their dalliance soon and get back to town. He didn't care what they did as long as they brought the berries Elk Heart wanted—and a semblance of sanity. The drought made everyone testy. The sight of the band of Arapahos riding into town had turned the citizens of Dehydration crazy.

Slocum pushed his way through the crowd until he got to the side of the chief's horse. He looked up at the man.

"Sorry the greeting got out of hand," Slocum said. "They're just too eager to see you and weren't expecting you until tomorrow."

"We ride fast," the chief said. "Elk Heart wants to start quick."

"He is a great and wise medicine man," Slocum allowed. "He knows when it's best for such things." Behind him Slocum heard the crowd still grumbling and felt the rifles trained not only on the Arapahos but on him.

"Where do we camp?"

"We'll find a spot outside town and—"

"In town. We camp in town," insisted the chief. "Such powerful medicine needs to be close."

"All right, we'll find a place." Slocum looked around for a friendly face in the crowd but saw none. It hadn't been that long since the Arapaho and the Cheyenne had raided constantly throughout Wyoming and Colorado. Most of the residents in Dehydration had probably lost a family member or friend to those raids. Memories were long and tempers short.

"Not in our town, they won't camp. No, sir," said a rail-thin man with a long scraggly beard. He clutched a rifle and looked determined to keep the Indians out of town, even if it meant massacring them here and now.

"They won't bother you," Slocum said. "I'll vouch for them. Tahlmann will, too."

"Where is that old coot? Out with the widder woman, prob'ly," the thin man said. Slocum marvelled at how few secrets there were in a town this size.

"You hold your horses, Joshua," came Tahlmann's brusque voice. "Don't go spreadin' rumors that aren't true 'bout your betters."

Tahlmann held up two large sacks.

"Didn't know how many chokeberries you'd need," he said to Elk Heart, "so I brought enough. And juniper berries, too." Tahlmann held up the second burlap sack. "Took me all afternoon of *hard work* gatherin' these, Joshua. All damn afternoon. What you been doin', other than insultin' our guests?"

"Guests! They're Arapahos!"

"And Elk Heart there is gonna do a rain dance and bring

water back. That makes him our friend, not somebody to threaten with a rifle. You ain't cleaned that rifle in a year, and it'd've blown up in your face."

"Cleaned it a couple months back," Joshua said sullenly.

"When you bought that gun oil?"

"Yeah, then."

"That was a year ago April."

"What's all the argument over?" Heads turned to stare at Madelaine Villareal. Slocum couldn't blame them since he stared, too. She had dressed and managed to keep the wrinkles out of her clothing. Even more surprising, her hair was neatly combed, unlike the shambles it had been after they'd made love.

"Slocum here's convinced an Arapaho medicine man to do a rain dance," said Tahlmann. "Good to see you back, Miss Villareal," he finished.

Slocum had suspected Maddy had made a reputation for herself earlier, left and then returned, but this confirmed it. Tahlmann greeted her warmly and the others in the crowd obviously knew her from the way they whispered among themselves. He only wished he could hear what they were saying.

"I thought he had more sense than that," Maddy said, sniffing. "I can't imagine he would believe in such a . . . such a superstition!"

Her vehemence startled him.

"There's no harm in trying," Slocum said. "And the peddler, Professor Leonardo, recommended Elk Heart."

"An itinerant snake oil salesman recommended a charlatan. Isn't that a fine kettle of fish," she said. "You know what's needed, Mr. Tahlmann."

"There's room for everyone, Miss Villareal."

"Call me Maddy. The days of me being 'Miss Villareal' ended when—" She abruptly bit off the explanation. Slocum was the only one who didn't understand.

"Sorry, ma'am, but breakin' the habit might be hard for

me," Tahlmann said. Slocum wanted to ask the man what he meant but found himself caught between the Indians and the crowd again.

"There're plenty of empty buildings, down the street and across from the abandoned laundry. I'll see that the Arapahos are settled in there. The rest of you can keep away."

"When's he gonna start hoppin' 'n dancin'?" asked Joshua. "The sooner he starts, might be the sooner we get some rain."

Slocum saw the calculation in the old medicine man's eyes and knew the Arapaho wasn't going to string them along. He wasn't disappointed when Elk Heart spoke.

"Tomorrow. Sundown tomorrow. That is when the Great Spirit will accept my dance."

"They'll need food and water while they're camped," Slocum said.

"Need much water," Elk Heart insisted.

"For the dance to be a success," Slocum hastily said when he saw the townspeople getting riled. "Tahlmann will give you a list of everything Elk Heart needs. And he'll tell you what they're to be paid."

More gumbling rose, then died out. Slocum wanted a chance to talk with Maddy, but she and Tahlmann left arm in arm, chatting like old friends. Slocum reckoned they were. It certainly explained how she was familiar with where everything was in town and how she had unerringly chosen one room in the boarding house over another.

He still didn't understand why she had chosen as she did, but he knew she had arrived at the decision long before going upstairs. For his part, he wouldn't mind renting the western room just to be close to the woman. He doubted Mrs. Jenkins would ever allow such a thing under her roof, however, no matter that she and Tahlmann were obviously enjoying one another's company without the benefit of marriage.

Slocum frowned and tried to figure out what Maddy had meant when she'd said, "So there, you son of a bitch." She hadn't minded what they had just done, not when she had wanted more when they were done, but Slocum had the feeling the words were not aimed at him. But who were they for?

"Show us campground," the Arapaho chief demanded.

Slocum looked around, then pointed to a spot a few yards away. It wasn't being used and all the buildings around the lot were abandoned. The area suited Elk Heart just fine from the way the medicine man walked about, grunting and shaking an eagle-feather–festooned rattle at each corner of the open space. He finally came back and nodded once.

"Good. Rain dance tomorrow. Sundown."

Slocum wished the Arapaho medicine man would do it now, but he had no idea what rituals were necessary to prepare for the actual dance.

"You give me whiskey" asked Elk Heart. "Need whiskey."

Slocum started to turn down the request, then decided a pint wasn't going to cause undue problems, and it would keep the Indians reasonably content.

"I'll be back in an hour, after you've set up camp."

Elk Heart grunted and began speaking to the hunting chief so fast Slocum missed even the intent, but there seemed to be no problems with the Indians. He hoped there would be none with the townspeople.

An hour after he returned and gave the pint to Elk Heart, Slocum went looking for Maddy, only to find she had turned in. Mrs. Jenkins was adamant about keeping him out, so Slocum went to the stables and bedded down in the stall next to his Appaloosa. It wasn't the same as being in a feather bed with Maddy Villareal, but it had to do.

Slocum awoke to the sound of a drum pounding a rhythmic, mournful beat. He sat bolt upright, his hand resting on the butt of his Colt. It took him several seconds to identify the sound and realize the Arapaho were banging away at a drum. He stretched, got to his feet and went out to see what the ruckus was.

It was barely sunrise and the Indians were seated in a large circle. In the middle Elk Heart danced slowly, moving this way and that as the drummers guided him in some fashion, speeding up and then slowing the tempo.

"So they started, eh? You reckon them boys'll bring rain?" asked Pete Tahlmann.

Slocum looked toward the mountains to the west. His eyes widened at the sight of wispy clouds forming over the highest peaks.

"Getting something where there's been nothing but empty blue sky. Elk Heart must have started early because the Great Spirit told him the time was right." What Slocum actually thought was that the Indians worried about how long they would be safe surrounded by the skeptical, hostile citizens of Dehydration if they hung around for an entire day.

Or maybe the time *was* nigh.

"You're right," Tahlmann said. "Think I ought to get those twenty horses ready for them?"

"Couldn't hurt. And get horses that don't mind being out in the rain," Slocum said. Tahlmann laughed and started to leave the spectacle of the Arapaho rain dance. As he started away Slocum had to ask, "Where's Miss Villareal?"

"I don't rightly know, though I can guess where she's not."

"Where's that?" Slocum asked. He watched the clouds thickening and forming a leaden underbelly.

"She'll tell you what she wants you to know. Not my place to speak on it," Tahlmann said. "But you're lookin' in the right direction for the answer."

Slocum stared at the storekeeper's back as he ambled off. Then he looked back into the mountains, wondering what Tahlmann meant. It was just one more mystery locked within the decreasing populace of Dehydration.

Another hour passed and Elk Heart danced steadily. The drummers tired and others took up the beat but the medicine man never slowed. Slocum had to admit the dance appeared to work. The clouds formed along the mountain ridge as far as he could see. And if he used a tad of imagination, he even saw lightning in those clouds, a testimony to their potential for releasing a downpour.

Slocum drifted away from the circle of hunters and began going through town hunting for Maddy. Everyone had seen her already that morning but no one knew where she was. And the citizens of the town were even more closemouthed than Pete Tahlmann about the woman. The best he got was from Mrs. Jenkins who scoffed at Maddy's reason for returning.

"She'll never get it to work, never in a million years," the woman declared.

No amount of coaxing could get her to reveal what she meant. Slocum gave up trying and after noon returned to the rain dance. Elk Heart danced as strongly as ever, though lines of fatigue on his ancient face betrayed the concentration he put into the ritual. Slocum saw that most of the citizens of the town had gathered around, many of them pointing at the thick clouds now slipping down the eastern slopes of the mountains and moving toward them.

"Looks like rain," Tahlmann said, sniffing. He puffed on a cigar and began pushing through the crowd, talking to several people at a time. All of them looked at the approaching storm.

If Slocum had bet on the outcome of the rain dance he would have lost. All they lacked was water hitting them in their upturned faces.

He turned from the mountains to the Indians when they began drumming faster. Elk Heart sped around the circle, digging a trench with his shuffling, dancing feet. He began chanting hoarsely, his voice almost gone from the constant ritualist song.

Slocum jumped at a sudden loud noise. He, like so many of the others, thought it was thunder. A second echo came, and he knew it was a gunshot. Spinning, his hand went to his holstered six-shooter, but he did not draw when he saw a cowboy galloping through town, firing wildly. Slocum had seen a drunken cowpoke hurrah a town more than once in his day, and the best solution to the problem was to let him ride on and hope he ran out of bullets before he hit somebody.

Then came more shots, and he knew this was no isolated event. Slocum drew, cocked his six-gun and aimed, only to have his hand batted up.

"No, don't," Pete Tahlmann warned. "It'll only cause trouble."

"It'll cause more trouble if they kill somebody," Slocum said.

"It's only Trent Campbell and his boys lettin' off steam."

A half dozen cowboys wheeled their horses in tight circles, kicking up a dust cloud that obscured them and the rest of Dehydration. Through the brown cloud rode a solitary man astride a massive white stallion.

Slocum slid his pistol back into his holster when he recognized Trent Campbell. Tahlmann had been right as to the culprit causing the ruckus.

"You put a muzzle on your men, Campbell!" shouted Tahlmann. "You can't go around shootin' up the town like this!"

"Why not? It's my town, even if you saw fit to rename it."

"You lost all right to this here town when you cut off our water," Tahlmann said hotly.

"What you got going on, Pete? A bunch of crazy Indians doing a war dance?" Campbell rode closer. Elk Heart had stopped his rain dance, and the others formed a tight knot, hands on their knives. Slocum saw that the hunting chief was edging toward their rifles stacked nearby.

"You interrupted Elk Heart," Tahlmann said.

"Hell, interrupt them some more, men!" Campbell waved to his cowboys. "Don't let them redskins infest my town!"

This set off a fight that Slocum knew no one would win. The men on the ground began grabbing at Campbell's mounted cowboys. Gunshots echoed, replacing the steady beat of Elk Heart's drummer with a constant report. Slocum tried to get to Trent Campbell. If he could reach the Circle C owner he could force him to call off his men. And if he couldn't, he'd at least vent his own anger by beating Campbell's face to a pulp.

Slocum tried but stopped when the crowd surged in front of him. He turned to skirt it, to find a different way to reach Campbell when he saw Maddy Villareal some distance away. Waving and shouting at her to get to safety failed to draw her attention. She stared at someone behind the bank building.

From the way she stood Slocum feared the worst. Maddy looked on the verge of running but was held in place by fear. He bounced off the crowd and went to help her when he saw Marsh Campbell ride out from behind the bank.

"Maddy!" Slocum shouted. She never turned. Her full attention fixed on Marsh.

The Circle C owner's son rode to her and bent low until their faces were only a foot apart. They were both talking at the same time, and from all Slocum could see, Maddy was angry. He couldn't get a good reading on Marsh Campbell's mood but from the set to his body, the man might reach out and strike the woman at any instant. Slocum drew his six-shooter and ran for them.

"Maddy!" he cried again. This time she heard him. The lovely dark-haired woman spun, saw him coming, then stepped back quickly from Marsh Campbell. Campbell sat upright in the saddle, with a look on his face sour enough to curdle milk. He reached for his six-gun, then saw that Slocum was slowing to take a bead on him. Campbell jerked hard on his horse's reins, wheeled around and galloped off in a thick cloud of dust.

"Are you all right?" Slocum asked, reaching Maddy's side. He spun around to find Campbell, but the young man had vanished.

"No thanks to him," Maddy spat out. "How can he—oh!" She angrily jerked free of Slocum's grip on her arm and stormed off. He watched her for a moment, then decided she wouldn't be in any danger. The real trouble was behind him. Increasing gunfire told him somebody was going to die unless cooler heads prevailed.

Slocum was at a loss to figure who that might be.

The crowd surged and struck out with fists and rocks, and the cowboys kicked and used their spurs as they fired over the heads of the crowd.

"All right, boys, let's head for home. It doesn't look like we're wanted around here," boomed Trent Campbell. The Circle C owner laughed harshly, rounded up his men and led them from town.

"Dangnabit," Pete Tahlmann said, nursing skinned knuckles from the fight. "If we had a marshal, Campbell'd be rotting in jail now. Him and all his men."

"Including his son," Slocum added.

"Marsh? Didn't see him," Tahlmann said.

Slocum said nothing. He'd have to talk to Maddy later about what Marsh Campbell's intentions had been. It wouldn't surprise Slocum to find the man had tried to kidnap her.

Slocum stood with his six-shooter drawn, then shoved it back. For a moment something bothered him and he couldn't put his finger on it. Then he realized there was utter silence. No drums, no gunfire, no chanting or distant thunder. He turned toward the mountains and saw the clouds breaking up and the afternoon sun shining through them.

"No rain today," Tahlmann said.

"No rain," Elk Heart said. "Break up magic. No rain ever."

"You're not going to start your dance again?" asked Slocum.

"Magic gone. Never return. Not here." Elk Heart stood with his arms crossed. The chief came up beside him, his rifle resting in the crook of his arm and looking as dour.

"We want horses," the chief said.

"What horses? You didn't make it rain," Tahlmann said.

"Give them the damned horses," Slocum said tiredly. "Elk Heart had the clouds forming. We all saw them. It's not his fault Campbell and his vermin chased away the spell—and the clouds."

Tahlmann looked at Slocum, then shook his head.

"You got a strange notion of justice."

"It's only fair. Elk Heart did what he said he would. It's not his fault Campbell rode into town."

The Arapaho chief and medicine man both nodded once. The rest of their band crowded close to form a united front against the white eyes.

"Eddie, Jimmy, fetch the animals from the corral." Tahlmann waited until the two returned with the twenty head of horses. The Arapaho wasted no time throwing hackamores around the horses' necks and in getting on the trail out of town.

As Elk Heart rode past Slocum, he favored him with a broad wink. Slocum had to laugh. He touched the brim of his hat, watched the Arapaho ride away, then went back into Dehydration to find Madelaine Villareal. He had a lot of questions he wanted answered and if it wasn't going to rain, he might as well get the answers.

8

Slocum walked in the dust cloud made by the retreating cowboys on their way back up into the canyon to the west. By the time he reached the boardinghouse, he was fuming mad. He should never have kept his finger off the trigger. He could have shot Trent Campbell out of the saddle. Slocum wasn't sure he believed that the rain dance was working or that the old medicine man had any special power to draw down storms from higher up in the mountains, but Campbell's appearance had ruined any chance of finding out.

He wasn't worried about Dehydration losing twenty head of horses to the Indians for the abortive attempt to conjure up rain, but he felt that his pride had taken a hit. He had let Professor Leonardo convince him the Arapaho medicine man was capable of forming rain clouds and had, in turn, convinced Tahlmann and the rest of the townspeople. The failure rested on his shoulders.

And he wanted to find out more about Maddy Villareal. She was a fine looking woman but had hidden more from him than she had shown—and she had shown him plenty already.

He started up the path leading to the front door of Mrs.

Jenkins's boardinghouse but stopped when he saw Maddy sitting on a bale of hay at the paddock beside the house where horses were fed and watered. She didn't notice him. Her attention was fixed on the mountains to the west, as if she could see through rock, past the canyon and to the lush pastureland of the Circle C behind the dam.

"You lit out mighty fast," Slocum said. Maddy jumped.

"Oh, you startled me," she said, her hand moving to her throat. She relaxed and patted the spot on the hay bale beside her. "Sit down, John."

He dropped and felt her leg pressing against his. He almost backed away but stayed put.

"You're upset with me. Why's that, John?" She half turned to look at him.

"What was Marsh Campbell trying to do? Kidnap you?"

"Kidnap me?" Maddy almost spat the words. "He doesn't have the sand to do that."

"So what was he trying to say to you?"

"Nothing I wanted to hear," she said. "Are you jealous, John? Of Marsh Campbell? Of *Marsh*?"

"His pa was trying to shoot up the town, him and the rest of his company. I didn't want you getting hurt."

"How sweet," she said. Maddy heaved a deep sigh that caused her chest to rise and fall delightfully. "All Trent wanted was to see if that Indian was succeeding. He has a mean streak, Trent Campbell does. How I hate that man!"

"What does it matter to Campbell if Elk Heart made rain or not? He's already got the Sulphur River dammed up and is keeping it, no matter if it rains or stays bone dry."

"He's mean, I tell you. He wants to see the town blow away."

"You weren't any more excited about Elk Heart and his dance."

"Of course I wasn't. That's all nonsense, John. Singing and dancing and shaking rattles. How's that supposed to make it rain? It can't," she answered, not caring what he was going to say. He saw the flush coming to her cheeks and how passionate she was on the subject. Slocum suspected something more was on the way.

"Why'd you come back to Dehydration?" he asked.

"Is it so obvious I've returned to town, rather than coming here for the first time, like you?" She looked at him, her dark eyes wide and innocent. He knew she was anything but innocent.

"Folks around here know you. Tahlmann, Mrs. Jenkins, others. You seem to have been here long enough before to get riled up just seeing Marsh Campbell or his pa."

"John, I left, but came back when I heard about the reward."

"For making it rain?" Slocum wondered what she was getting at.

"No, no, that's not what the reward is for," she said, her passion returning. "The reward is for bringing water to Campbell—Dehydration," she hastily amended. "I can certainly use the money."

"Who couldn't?" Slocum thought a moment, then asked, "How do you intend to do it? Since I've been here, they've had men sending dynamite up in a balloon, a snake oil salesman with a Water Extract and an Arapaho medicine man doing a rain dance. It's not going to be too long before gunmen show up and ride into that canyon to kill Campbell, his men and anyone else trying to stop them so they can blow up the dam."

"The dam should never have been built," Maddy said, "but my method is proven. I want to get water for Tahlmann and everyone else still in town. Let Campbell keep his damned water!"

"How are you going to do this?"

"Not by hauling water from a sulfur pit out on the prairie," Maddy said. She moved even closer, her arm pressing intimately against his so she could lean and whisper in his ear. Slocum wondered if her secret was so dangerous she dared not let anyone overhear or if she simply wanted to distract him. If this was her reason, she succeeded. Her long, dark hair fluttered on the gentle wind blowing off the mountains and touched his cheek. He smelled her scent and became distracted by her touch and heat.

"Will you help me, John? But you've got to promise not to tell anyone what I'm doing until I have a secure source of water. A new well."

"It's not got anything to do with dancing?" Slocum asked. He had learned to never trust a woman who didn't like to dance or a man who did.

"I'll show you," she said. "Wait here. I'll change my clothing and be back in a few minutes."

"It'll be an eternity," Slocum said.

"Oh, John, you say the sweetest things." Maddy kissed him lightly on the cheek, then got to her feet and rushed off. Slocum knew she was in a hurry because she didn't bother brushing off the hay clinging to her skirt.

He expected Maddy to take the rest of the day changing, but she surprised him. Less than fifteen minutes later she returned, carrying a small black leather case that reminded Slocum of a doctor's bag.

"You in a hurry?" Slocum asked.

"I want the money, John," she said. But he heard more than simple greed in her tone. She wanted to prove something, but what that was he was at a loss to say.

"Where are we headed?"

"I've done a study of the area," she said, taking out a rolled-up map from the small case. She opened it on the hay bale and studied the contour lines for a moment. "Here is the spot." Her finger stabbed down.

Slocum looked at the map, then straightened and got his bearings.

"About a mile north of town," he said. "What are we going to find there?"

"Water," she said. "Water. Let's go."

"It'll be dark in a spell," he said.

"That doesn't matter."

Slocum found himself more curious than anything else about Maddy's quest to find water in the middle of the prairie. As far as he could tell from the map, there wasn't any trace of water in the area. The dry riverbed for the Sulphur River was some distance off.

Suddenly, Maddy drew rein and looked around when they had reached the area she had indicated earlier. As far as Slocum could tell, there was no hope to find water.

"I'll start here," Maddy said, slipping to the ground. She opened her case. Slocum thought she was hunting for her map, but she took out a Y-shaped branch.

"What's that?" he asked.

"A birch dowsing rod," she said. "I'm going to find water by dowsing." She held the twig by the shorter branches and let the longer segment point out across the empty, arid prairie.

"What—?"

"Hush, John. I need to concentrate." She closed her eyes and held the divining rod at arm's length in front of her. Slowly turning, she returned to her original position. Slocum started to say something about her failure when the rod jiggled and jerked, pulling her back to the east.

Slocum dismounted and tethered their horses. By the time he caught up with Maddy, she was a dozen yards off, walking slowly and being pulled along by the dowsing rod. She walked as if she were sleepwalking, so Slocum did nothing to disturb her.

Maddy turned slightly and walked with a steadier stride. Slocum kept a sharp eye out on the ground to be sure she wasn't stepping on a prairie rattler or into a gopher hole. Mostly, though, he simply trailed her in wonder. He had doubted Elk Heart's rain dance would work and had been surprised to see the clouds forming after a few hours of chanting and dancing. Not for an instant had he believed Professor Leonardo's or Ballantine's wild claims. He wasn't sure what to make of Maddy claiming to be able to witch water.

Back in Georgia he had seen a man locate a well using a switch cut off a birch tree. Whenever Slocum's pa had wanted something found he had always asked the man to come out to the Stand and work his magic. Slocum saw no reason for it to work, but then he saw no reason that it shouldn't.

"It's getting stronger, John. It's almost jumping out of my hands," Maddy said excitedly. "There's water nearby. I know it!" She almost ran as she rushed across the prairie. Slocum looked back over his shoulder in the direction of their horses. Although they were alone as far as he could see, he worried about leaving the horses.

"We ought to get the horses and come back here and pick up the search."

"I feel it, John. I *feel* it! I'm not going to break the spell." Maddy jerked about as if pulled by the dowsing rod and ran now. Slocum puffed as he ran to keep up with her.

"How much farther?" he asked after a few minutes of this headlong rush toward . . . what?

Slocum almost ran into the woman when she abruptly stopped. He saw that the tip of the divining rod pointed straight down. It was getting dark but enough daylight remained for Slocum to see the area clearly.

"This is it. Water's below."

"How do we get to it?" Slocum looked around for some sign that the vegetation grew faster or turned greener because of a subterranean pool.

"I don't know that, John. It's here, though." Maddy sweat profusely. She wiped it from her forehead using her sleeve. "What's the usual way of getting water? Drilling?"

"Drill here? Why here and not over there or back in town? It costs a fortune to put up a drill rig," Slocum said.

"We dig here because the water is below. I know it."

"I didn't bring a shovel," Slocum said, trying to keep the sarcasm from his voice and failing. "Look around," he continued, cutting off Maddy's angry response. "There's nothing greener here than anywhere else. The roots on some mesquite in Texas grow straight down a hundred feet or more to find water, and the mesquite leaves are green. But everything here is dead or dying."

"I don't care. There's water here."

Slocum saw that Maddy was not going to give up easily. He began scouting the area for any sign that she might be right. A few yards away he stopped to examine the ground. Twilight hid much of the detail, but the area was rockier than the rest. He dropped to his knees and began pulling away the fist-sized stones stacked here.

"What did you find, John?"

"Maybe nothing, but—" Slocum let out a cry as the ground gave way under him. He fell several feet and slammed hard into the ground. As he looked up, he caught a shower of dirt and pebbles in the face. He threw up his arm to shield himself and turned.

"Are you all right, John? Tell me!"

"I'm all right," Slocum said, getting to his feet. He took a step, turned his ankle and fell heavily. Twisting around, he saw the woman silhouetted against the darkened sky. "Watch your step. I fell about ten feet."

"Do you need help getting out?"

"Let me look around. I never suspected this hole was even here." Slocum got to his feet painfully and limped a few feet on his turned ankle. It might swell a mite but wasn't going to slow him. He fumbled a lucifer from the tin in his pocket and struck it. The sudden flare of light dazzled him for an instant, then gave him a good view of where he had fallen.

Roots dangled down from above, all dried and dying.

The walls of the cavern crumbled as Slocum brushed past, causing him to back away.

"Maddy, get my horse and a rope to pull me out," he called. There wasn't any answer. Slocum snuffed out the lucifer and went back to the hole where he had fallen into the tunnel. "Maddy!"

A cascade of dirt blinded him an instant before he was bowled over. He and Maddy thrashed about in the dirt until he called out, "Stop! Stop fighting me. I want to get untangled."

"I scraped my elbows and knees," the woman complained.

"We might be in a lot worse trouble if we can't get back out of here."

"That's not a problem, John."

Slocum lit another lucifer and saw what she meant. The side of the hole had collapsed completely, leaving a steeply sloping path back to the prairie. With a little scrambling they could get back to solid ground and their horses.

He helped Maddy to her feet. She brushed off dirt and then examined her elbows. Without a hint of modesty, she hiked her skirts high and looked at her bloodied, bruised knees. About this time the lucifer burned out again, forcing Slocum to toss it aside as it scorched his fingers.

"I'm a mess," she said.

"You found this tunnel," Slocum said. "It looks like the Sulphur River or some other underground water flow usually fills it. But the drought has dried it up. You found a dry hole."

"I don't believe that for a minute," Maddy said primly. "You said it yourself. Water flowed here. Recently, too. That means we can find the source and get all the water the people in Campbell—Dehydration—could want."

"There hasn't been water here in a while," Slocum said, kicking at the floor. He knelt and pressed his hand down past the dry layer. It was muddy below.

"See?" Maddy cried in triumph. "There's mud. That means there must be water."

"There has been," Slocum said.

"We need a torch to light the way. And if you won't come along, *I* need a torch."

Slocum gave in to the inevitable and began gathering piles of dried roots and some grass to ignite the torch. He found some green roots and added them to the bundle, rubbing mud over the driest ones to keep them from flaring and then burning quickly to an ash.

"Let's give it a try," Slocum said. He lit another lucifer and shied away as the torch flared. It let off clouds of dense smoke as it burned fitfully.

"Good enough to see," Maddy said, coughing from the smoke.

"What are we looking for?" he asked.

"What stopped the water? There must be a dam here, just like the one Trent Campbell built to shut off water to Dehydration."

Resolute, Maddy Villareal started walking. She was short enough not to have to duck to miss the low hanging roots. Slocum's six-foot height proved inconvenient within a hundred paces as the tunnel roof lowered. He had to walk bent over, letting the smoke fill his nostrils and choke him. His eyes watered, but he kept pace with Maddy as she plowed ahead.

"Finding anything?" he called.

"Evidence of water flowing through here recently. This must be what the dowsing rod detected."

Slocum didn't know for certain but he had the feeling the floor sloped down as they walked, increasing the distance back to the surface. He had worked in mines and being underground didn't spook him like it did some men, but he had a gut feeling that the unsupported old water channel wasn't getting any safer.

"The torch is burning out," Slocum called. "Let's go back so we can get the proper equipment to explore."

"Proper equipment?" asked Maddy.

"Miner's carbide lamp, maybe miner's candles or a dozen pitch torches if we can't find the lamps." Slocum knew better than to order the woman to leave. She was like a bloodhound on a scent and wasn't going to quit, but he had given her incentive to leave—coming back so she could delve even farther underground in her quest for water.

And the $5000 reward offered by the town.

"The tunnel goes on forever," Maddy said.

"All the more reason to bring proper equipment. And some supplies. I'm mighty thirsty and don't want to squeeze water out of the mud to get a good drink."

"You can do that?" she asked.

Slocum started to answer but the ground shook. He staggered into Maddy and they both fell. A blast of dust from behind rolled over them, covering them and snuffing the air from their lungs.

9

Slocum heard muffled sounds he couldn't identify. Then the ground under him began to move, to struggle, to hit him with fists. Shock flowed away as he realized he had landed on top of Maddy and the sounds he heard were her crying for him to move. The fists were hers, too, forcing him to let her breathe.

"Are you in one piece?" he asked.

"No, thanks to you. I almost got crushed."

"We both almost did," Slocum said. The torch lay where he had dropped it, sputtering and sizzling like fat dropped in a fire. The faint light it still cast showed the tunnel behind them was plugged.

"What happened?" Maddy asked.

"The channel is usually filled with water. That supports the weaker spots in the roof. No water, no support and it fell. Whether we did anything to cause it or if it was just ready because of the long dry spell, I don't know."

"What does it matter?" Maddy scrambled to her feet and almost shouted. "What does it matter why it fell? We're trapped!"

Slocum sat with his back to the wall. His feet still found

mud but there wasn't room enough above for him to stand without banging his head.

"What are we going to do? We're trapped!"

"First thing, we settle down." Slocum slowly got his wits back.

"Easy for you to say. How many times have you almost died?" Maddy was quieting down, but Slocum saw she fought hard to keep from panicking.

"A few times," Slocum allowed, "but this isn't one of them."

"What are you saying?"

"The torch isn't sputtering and sparking any worse than it was before. We've still got enough air. Might be trapped in the tunnel ahead of us, but we have enough so we won't suffocate."

"But food. Water," Maddy said.

"I can get you some water. Won't taste good, but I can get you a mouthful or two." Slocum took off his bandanna and scooped up a handful of mud. He tied the ends of the bandanna and began squeezing the bandanna until drops of water formed. "Get down, flat on your back."

"John, really!"

"You want water or not?" He held the bandanna higher so she could see the droplet threatening to fall unsampled.

"Very well, but it sounded as if . . ."

"Anything wrong with that?" he asked, smiling.

"Nothing. Oh, that's so tasty," Maddy said sarcastically, turning her head aside and acting as if she wanted to spit.

"But it's wet."

Slocum continued dripping water into her mouth until she had enough to wet her lips, then used the same technique to sample the bitter, dirty water himself. It wasn't much of a filter, but it served its purpose. He felt better after he had milked the mud of almost a mouthful of water.

"Now what do we do?" Maddy asked.

"From what I can see, getting back the way we came isn't likely." Slocum got to his feet and poked at the top of the cave-in. There wasn't any hint of air coming through and he didn't see that moving the mountain of dirt would gain them anything. He had no idea how far back the cave-in extended, either. If they were lucky, they could get to the surface fast, but Slocum still had the feeling they were far underground. The tunnel had sloped downward for a considerable distance from where they had so unceremoniously entered it.

Going back was out of the question. That meant they had to continue. But the tunnel still sloped down.

"We've got to make tracks," Slocum said. "The torch is burning itself out."

"We might stay and dig," Maddy said uneasily.

"Or you might use that diving rod of yours to find a way out," he said.

"How?"

Slocum hesitated. He had spoken in anger, but the notion that she had found this tunnel meant she had some ability using the birch stick to find things that were hidden.

"Weak spots in the roof," he said. "Can you divine the weakest spot so we can dig there?"

"We're only going to get one chance to escape, aren't we?"

"Looks like it," Slocum said. "The cave-in might be where we go. Try the divining rod."

Maddy looked frightened. The guttering light from the torch cast strange shadows on her high-boned cheeks, giving her the look of some supernatural creature. She fumbled a little as she took out the Y-shaped dowsing rod and held it in shaking hands.

"I've never looked for anything but water."

"You found a tunnel. I've heard of dowsers finding pipes. That's nothing but a hollow spot in the ground, if you think on it."

"I can only try," she said. Closing her eyes, Maddy stood stock-still for several minutes, then turned and began walking—farther into the tunnel. Slocum took a last look at the dirt plugging the way back and quickly followed the woman as she hastened along the tunnel. She went deeper, ever deeper into the bowels of the earth.

Slocum tasted water now in the humid, trapped air. Then he saw how the tunnel floor slanted up slightly. He also saw that the roof changed from dirt with roots dangling down to more substantial rock. They were reaching the foothills. The tunnel walls became rock worn smooth by the endless rush of water in the subterranean channel. Digging free through solid rock wasn't possible. Even if he had dynamite, he could never blast through it. But Maddy pressed on.

As the torch spat forth the last of its febrile sparks the woman stopped and looked straight up.

"Here," she said. "Here's where it points."

Slocum thrust the torch over his head and found a cavity that stretched farther than the dying sparks from the torch could illuminate.

"It's dark," she said, a catch in her voice.

"Mighty dark," Slocum allowed. He dropped the burned-out torch and put his arms around her. She came to him easily and pressed her face against his chest. He felt her shuddery sobs for a moment, then she quieted.

"We'd better start digging. How are we going to do it?"

"I saw a couple rocks to my right where I can stand and maybe reach high enough to find the roof. But the digging'll have to be done with my fingers. We don't have anything else."

"I'll do what I can."

"I know," Slocum said, hoping that she had already done her job by finding a spot where they might have a chance of escape. He moved away from her, found the rocks and carefully climbed atop them.

Then began the hard part. In complete darkness, he reached up until he found the roof at the top of the cavity. Tracing out large rocks with his fingertips, he guessed what it looked like and began tugging at the stones most likely to open another few inches toward the surface. He worked for what seemed an eternity; his arms turned to lead and he wobbled as he reached for ever higher stones.

Slocum pried loose an especially large rock and then tumbled to the floor when he lost his balance.

"John! John!" Maddy cried. "Did you hurt yourself?"

"I'm fine," he said, sucking in a deep breath. It took him a second to realize what had changed. The humid, close air now tasted like fresh air blowing across the Wyoming prairie. He rolled onto his back and stared straight up and saw stars.

"We did it! We broke out!"

Slocum wondered at their luck—or Maddy's skill with the diving rod. It didn't matter what had brought them to this point. They were free.

"There's not a bone in my body that doesn't ache," Madelaine Villareal declared as they rode into Dehydration just before dawn. "All I want is a hot bath and to sleep for a week. No, not a week, a month."

"We can get the gear and explore the rest of the tunnel," Slocum said, more to tease her than from any desire on his part.

"That's true," she said thoughtfully. "Perhaps I won't sleep a week, after all. A bath and I'll be ready to go back. Can you get the lamps and whatever else we'd need?"

"Whoa," he said. "I need a bath, too, and there's not much water in these parts. And I need to sleep." He considered how tired he was and the notion of going to bed with Maddy didn't even excite him at the moment. All he wanted was to sleep.

"Be like that," she said tartly, then laughed. "Oh, John, it is so much fun teasing you. You take everything so seriously."

"You were, too, when we were buried alive. That tunnel might have been our grave."

"There's water at the end. There has to be. That's why the diving rod showed me how to get in."

"Take your bath. I'll come by later," Slocum said.

"Not too much later," Maddy said, bending over and giving him a wet kiss on his grimy cheek. She trotted away as if she didn't have a care in the world.

Slocum walked his Appaloosa slowly to the stables and put the horse into a stall. The stableman was nowhere to be seen, so Slocum tended his horse, made sure plenty of food and a bucket of water was within easy reach, then flopped into the next stall, not even bothering to lay down his blanket. His dreams were more like nightmares: trapped underground, drowned, crushed, and all with Maddy reaching out to him—her fingers just beyond his grasp.

Sometime in the late afternoon, he awoke. Heat boiled in, but it had been the dreams that brought him out of his sleep. Slocum rubbed his eyes, then got up and tended his horse again. There was still no trace of the stableman, so Slocum tended the other three horses in the stalls before going to find himself some food. His belly growled and the drink he had taken from the horse's water bucket didn't go far to quench his thirst.

As he walked out into the main street, he looked around. Activity was at an ebb, even for Dehydration in the middle of a hot, dry summer. Nowhere did anyone stir. He sauntered to the restaurant and went in, hoping it would be open. At the rear of the dining area a well-dressed, portly man argued with another dressed in a white apron. Slocum couldn't hear what was going on, but he caught the gist of the matter.

The one was a banker wanting money that the restaurant owner didn't have.

"Please, Mr. Harlow. You can't foreclose like this. There's no business anywhere in town. It's the drought."

"You got till the end of the month," the portly man said, slipping his thumbs into the armholes of his vest and poking out his ample belly. For a second, Slocum thought the banker was going to bump the café owner out of the way. Instead, he let out a deep-throated "harumph" and stalked out.

"You open for business?" Slocum asked.

"Reckon so, but not for long. Business has been slack, and he wants his money."

"The bank's foreclosing on you?"

"The bank? Hell, no, Eustace Harlow is foreclosing. He gets a sick thrill out of seeing men squirm."

"I'll put a dollar into your pocket if you can fix me up with a meal."

"Whatever you want. Slocum, ain't it?"

Slocum dropped a silver cartwheel on the table, then added another when he was done with the best meal he'd eaten since leaving Omaha. His only complaint about the food was lack of coffee with it. There wasn't enough water to boil coffee, and Slocum had to settle for gulping down the food the best he could.

"You don't have to give me anything extra, Slocum," the owner said.

"Keep it. Put it toward what you owe Harlow."

"Won't matter. You keep it. Get yourself something to wet your whistle at the saloon." The second silver dollar flashed through the air. Slocum snared it easily and tucked it away.

"Things might be changing around here soon," he told the man.

"Won't be soon enough. Purty near everyone's left town and that son of a bitch Harlow is buying up property hand over fist. Heard-tell he'd bought the livery stables when Fred left."

Slocum suspected that he would be evicted from the stall where he slept when Harlow got around to tending to the business of running the stables.

"As long as he doesn't own the saloon and make everyone pay double," Slocum said.

"He's likely to do just that. He wouldn't piss in your mouth if your guts was on fire."

Slocum stepped back out into the hot Wyoming afternoon and swiped at sweat running down his face. He had washed out his bandanna, but it was still dirty, so he just used his hand. Turning toward the saloon for the drink he had missed out on in the restaurant, he stopped and stared when he saw a rider making his way westward behind the saloon.

"Marsh Campbell," Slocum muttered. He flipped the leather thong off the hammer of his six-shooter and lengthened his stride to overtake Trent Campbell's son. By the time he got around the saloon Campbell had vanished. But Slocum had a notion where he'd headed. Running, he went to Mrs. Jenkins's boardinghouse.

On the same hay bale where Slocum had met Maddy the day before sat Marsh Campbell—and next to him was the beautiful woman. Slocum started to call out, but he saw that they were arguing again. Now and then Marsh pointed to the west, in the direction of the dammed up canyon. Whatever he said, Maddy wanted none of it. She shoved him hard enough to knock him off the end of the bale. Marsh fell to the ground, sat up and pointed in the direction of the Circle C ranch again. Then he got to his feet, pulled his hat down around his ears, mounted his horse and galloped off.

Slocum hung back, watching Maddy closely. She stood, as if she was going to call after him. Then she made an obscene gesture and stormed back into the boardinghouse. Slocum hurried back to the stables, saddled his Appaloosa and was on the trail going after Marsh before Maddy had time to reach her east-facing room on the second floor.

Slocum had a good idea where Marsh headed and threw caution to the winds. The younger man never looked back and made no effort to hide his trail. As Slocum rode, he argued with himself what to do when he caught Marsh. Mostly, Slocum wanted answers the young man could give and they were all about Madelaine Villareal.

Ride as he did, though, Slocum lost Marsh Campbell along the road leading into the canyon. When he came to the towering canyon walls, he slowed and then reined back, looking around. He saw nothing, but more important, he heard nothing. Wherever Marsh had gone, it wasn't up the canyon toward the dam. The sound of his horse's hoofbeats would have echoed back.

Slocum retraced his path and found where Marsh Campbell had left the road, taking a narrow, rocky trail that lead up the side of the canyon to the rim. Here and there Slocum detected traces of recent passage. A sharp, shiny cut in a rock made by a steel horseshoe. Dislodged rocks. A plant that had been stepped on. Slocum dismounted and ran his fingers along the stem. Juice turned his fingers sticky. The plant had been broken off less than an hour ago.

If he judged times properly, Marsh would have ridden this way ten minutes ahead of him. Slocum considered the wisdom of remaining on the narrow path when Marsh had the high ground. If the young rancher stopped he would certainly see Slocum behind him on the trail.

That might not be too bad, Slocum figured. They were going to have it out sooner or later. On this rocky path was as good a place as any.

Slocum dismounted and led his Appaloosa upward but had not gone twenty yards when a bullet sang off the rock face of the canyon wall. He ducked, fought to keep his horse from rearing, then moved it to a spot where he could take a bit of shelter from the lead storm coming at him.

A single shot was followed by two or three, then a half dozen tore up the air. Almost as if a solitary gunman had to reload, there was a long pause only to have renewed fire replace the silence.

Marsh might have gone to the rim and summoned his father's guards. Or those guards might simply have spotted Slocum on their own. Letting an intruder slip by them into Circle C country would be a crime Trent Campbell would punish severely.

Slocum had a hard time even locating the hidden gunmen. Two might be ahead on the trail and another high on the rim. Or he might be entirely wrong. Unless he was certain where the snipers were, he would be entirely dead.

Tugging on his horse's reins he began a slow move back down the trail. When he rounded a bend and had the rock wall shielding him, he mounted and rode as if his life depended on it. If Trent Campbell had anything to say about it, Slocum's life probably did hang in the balance.

He returned to Dehydration after sundown and got the whiskey he had neglected earlier in the day, thinking hard as he knocked back one shot after another.

10

"Stupid," Slocum grumbled to himself as he took another drink. "I bulled in and didn't scout like I should have."

"What's that, Slocum?" asked the barkeep. "Didn't hear you. You want another?"

Slocum wobbled on his feet. He nodded, took the half bottle of whiskey and sat heavily in the chair near the door. He turned over and over everything he had done wrong that day and marvelled that he had not ended up as buzzard bait. Campbell's guards should have knocked him out of the saddle with their first shot.

"Maybe they only wanted to chase me off," he said. The barkeep looked at him strangely, as if he didn't see men talking to themselves that often. Slocum ignored him. The whiskey hit the spot. He took another swing from the bottle, not bothering to use the shot glass as an intermediary between the liquor and his mouth. The liquid burned all the way down, but by now Slocum was comfortably numb.

Since blundering into Dehydration, there hadn't been a whole lot that had gone right.

"Except for her," Slocum said, grinning foolishly. Maddy Villareal had been a bright spot. Even as the thought of the dark-haired, fiery beauty came to mind, a new picture replaced it. One with her and Marsh Campbell together.

"You got a minute, son?"

Slocum looked up, thinking someone spoke to him. The banker, Eustace Harlow, had entered the almost empty saloon and leaned on the bar. He stared straight at the bartender. The man looked around, as if he might find a way to escape, then screwed up his courage and went to stand in front of the banker.

"What'll it be, Mr. Harlow? Your usual?"

"Always remember the customer. I like that, Benjamin. I do. When you sell me this place, I'll keep you on, if you remember every customer's drink and can call them by name."

"Most I remember," the barkeep said.

"Excellent, Benjamin. You are good at what you do, just as I am good at what I do. I buy property. I want to buy your saloon."

"Not for sale, Mr. Harlow," the barkeep said. He licked his lips and started to back away as if he faced a hungry wolf ready to eat him alive.

Slocum wondered if that was so far from the truth. He saw Harlow's face reflected in the dirty mirror behind the bar and had seen friendlier grizzly bears.

"Any price I offer will be generous, Benjamin. There are no patrons any more. Five hundred dollars for everything."

"Everything, Mr. Harlow? But my stock's worth twice that. And the building, well, it's not the sturdiest, but it's worth more than—"

"Take the offer, son. It won't be on the table forever. If you wait too long, Dehydration will be a ghost town and you won't have anyone to peddle your rotgut to."

"He's got me," Slocum said. As he listened to the banker, he sobered up. A seething anger at what the man tried to do filled Slocum and burned away the fog of booze that had settled over his brain. "I may not be much, but I pay for what I get." Slocum flipped the silver dollar the restaurant owner had given back over to the barkeep. Benjamin fielded it easily and made a big show of going to the cash register and giving it a good crank, opening the drawer amid tingling bells, then dropping the coin into the tray before slamming it with gusto.

"Got me customers, Mr. Harlow. Now, what do you want? Your usual beer?"

"That's why you're not making a profit, Benjamin," Slocum said. "Cheap customers. A beer? Why not buy yourself a bottle of whiskey? You look like you could use it."

"I, sir, am not a cheap drunk."

"Nope, you don't look like a drunk," Slocum said.

"Are you implying I am cheap?" Harlow spun and faced Slocum.

Slocum stood, kicked back the chair and said, "I'm agreeing with you. Any problem with that?" Slocum studied Harlow more closely now than he had earlier. The man might be wearing a shoulder rig with a small caliber pistol tucked under his left arm. There might also be a hideout gun hidden in a side pocket or a derringer in a vest pocket. There was no way Harlow could drag a pistol out from any of those places before Slocum could clear leather.

The tension crackled between them, then Harlow backed down.

"Forgot the beer, Benjamin. And if you haven't taken my offer to buy this dump by noon tomorrow, forget the five hundred bucks, too." Harlow glowered at Slocum, then left.

"Sorry to run off half your trade," Slocum said, sitting back down. He stared at the whiskey still in the bottom. About an inch of the amber fluid remained. He pushed the bottle away. He'd swallowed enough for the night.

"Don't be, Slocum. Ever since the drought began, he's been tryin' to buy up danged near everything in town."

"Now why would a smart banker like Eustace Harlow

do a thing like that?" Slocum said aloud. "If he's right and Dehydration's destined to become a ghost town, what good would it do him?"

"The drought won't last forever. What else does he have to do with his money besides put in lowball offers for land and buildings that'll be a hundred times as much when we get rain again?"

"Or the Sulphur River is flowing once more," Slocum said.

"That's not likely to happen, not with the like of Trent Campbell sittin' on all our water."

"Reckon you're right," Slocum said, thinking the opposite. If Harlow and Campbell were in cahoots, this might be a land grab.

"Heard Harlow's bought most of the ranches around here, too. The Bar None won't sell, and there's not much Harlow can do about that since they don't have a loan with his bank. But everyone else around here is beholden to that damned bank."

"You're not, are you?"

"No, sir, I am not," Benjamin said proudly. "I paid for everything with cash and was successful enough, during the rainy years, at least, to pay all my bills without borrowing a dime. I'd cut my own throat 'fore I'd borrow from the likes of Mr. Harlow."

The barkeep looked closer at Slocum, then said, "You're lookin' to win that reward money Tahlmann's put up, aren't you, Slocum?"

"I'd be lying if I said that wasn't a mighty attractive sum," Slocum said. "Why?"

"I think there's a well out on the Newcombe place."

"So?"

"I heard-tell Harlow is putting real pressure on Mr. Newcombe to sell. Think Harlow might smell water there, too."

"Does this Newcombe fellow have any way of drilling to reach the water?"

"Nope. He's in debt up to his ears and Harlow's not likely to loan him a penny more."

"Sounds interesting," Slocum said. "Might be I should take a ride out there to look over the place."

"Tell Newcombe he's still got friends around town, no matter what Harlow might say."

Slocum looked at the rest of the whiskey in the bottle and knew he wasn't going to drink it now. But he wasn't going to waste it, either. He grabbed the bottle by the neck, shoved in the cork and left with the bottle. It might make the trail dust a little less gritty.

As he rode Slocum considered his motives for going out to the Newcombe spread. He had to laugh at his cockeyed optimism when he figured out that he was going to see if there might actually be a chance that water might be on the land. If he couldn't spot it using the obvious signs of greener vegetation or even swampy land, he might persuade Maddy to dowse and split the money with him.

And with Newcombe.

That was a good excuse, but Slocum knew it had more to do with taking an instant dislike to Eustace Harlow. He had seen men like Harlow profit too many times at the expense of men with more heart but less money or business experience. Worse, Slocum saw in Harlow a lot of the carpetbagger judge who had seized Slocum's land for nonpayment of taxes just after the war. The judge and his hired gunman had ridden out to seize the property that had belonged to the Slocum family since George I had deeded it over. The judge and his henchman had remained on the land after Slocum rode out that day—but they were in shallow graves near the spring house.

The road to the Newcombe place was well marked but Slocum rode past, then cut across the prairie to get a feel for the land. The view didn't look too promising. Nowhere did he see any evidence of water seeping up from below, not even sulfur-laden water. The plowed fields had no irrigation water after the Sulphur River had been dammed up, cutting off everyone below the Circle C. The few cows staggering around in a futile hunt for forage would have to be slaughtered soon to keep them from dying of dehydration or even outright starvation.

Maddy would have to be more than a water witch to find sustaining liquid here. She'd have to work miracles.

Slocum started back toward town. There wasn't any reason to talk with Newcombe when water wasn't available. But Slocum had barely reached the road when he heard a gunshot from the direction of the Newcombe house. He kept riding until a second shot sounded, followed quickly by a third and fourth. Turning his horse's face, he galloped across the prairie to reach the simple house as quickly as possible.

While he had been roaming about Newcombe's land, Harlow and two gunmen had ridden up. Slocum went cold inside as he remembered that day back in Calhoun, Georgia, with the carpetbagger judge. He reached across and slid the leather keeper off the hammer of his Colt Navy.

"You don't have any choice in the matter, Newcombe," Harlow said loudly. Slocum saw the banker intended to browbeat not only the man but his wife and two small children. All were grimy from lack of bathing, but even the filth could not hide their fearful expressions. Harlow's intimidation was working.

"Please, we can't—" Newcombe cut off his plea when Slocum rode up.

"Howdy," Slocum said. "I was passing by and heard gunfire. Any trouble here?"

"There's no trouble, Slocum," Harlow said coldly. "Ride on out so I can finish my business with these good people."

"You must be Newcombe," Slocum said, ignoring the banker. "Benjamin from in town said to give you his regards."

For the first time since he had been here, Slocum saw genuine admiration on Newcombe's face. The man smiled, showing a pair of broken teeth in front. But his happiness faded quickly when Harlow moved to stand between him and Slocum.

"I want your answer now. It's a fair offer."

"I wouldn't have anything to show for three years of workin' this place, Mr. Harlow," said Newcombe. His wife clutched at his sleeve, but Newcombe jerked free. Slocum saw the man had backbone and was going to tell Harlow what he could do with his insulting offer. He also saw how Harlow's two henchmen were reaching for their six-guns. Slocum had no idea who had fired before, but he was likely to find out mighty fast.

"Don't go swinging those six-shooters around, gents," Slocum said. "You might not like what happens."

"Get the hell out of here, Slocum," growled Harlow. "This is not your concern."

"If either of them goes for his six-shooter, it will be. I'd say it's mighty hard to think about business when two gun-slingers are pointing their irons at you."

Harlow turned and started to say something to his men. Slocum cleared leather and had his six-shooter aimed at the banker's head before the first word slipped from his lips.

"You talk a lot, but I think it's time you listened. What do you want to do, Mr. Newcombe?"

"He tried to run me off. Said he'd burn me out if I didn't accept his offer of a hunnerd dollars for the homestead."

"I'll have to burn off the dead crops and slaughter those worthless cows of yours," Harlow said, as if this explained why he offered almost nothing for a spread worth ten times as much.

"How much do you owe this snake in the grass?" Slocum asked. When Harlow bristled, he made a show of aiming his Colt directly at the banker's bulbous nose.

"Not even a hunnerd dollars," Newcombe said.

"He was going to take what you do owe out of the money he'd pay. Weren't you going to do that, Harlow?" Slocum saw the answer on the banker's face. Harlow intended to walk away with the deed paying only a few dollars and a cancelled mortgage.

"I'll help Newcombe negotiate, since he doesn't seem to have the firepower you do," Slocum said. His rock-steady grip gave no hint of wavering, and his cold eyes showed he was capable of pulling the trigger, if either of the banker's gunmen tried anything.

"I can foreclose on you, Newcombe. I'll do it and you won't get a dime!"

"What's it take to keep your mortgage current?" asked Slocum.

"Seven whole dollars, and I don't have it."

"Here," Slocum said, carefully pulling his wad of greenbacks from his pocket and using his thumb to roll off a twenty dollar bill. "Here's enough for three months."

"You're a dollar shy," Harlow said automatically.

"Newcombe will pay you the dollar in three months. Consider yourself lucky to have a fine loan holder who pays in advance."

When Harlow went to stuff the bill into his pocket, Slocum thrust out his six-shooter.

"Write the man a receipt. Be sure to put on it what the money's for. Three months mortgage—in advance!"

Harlow grumbled but did as he was ordered. He thrust the receipt at Newcombe as if it was on fire and he'd burn himself if he hung onto it an instant longer.

"This might get us into the rainy season," Newcombe said with almost pathetic excitement. "It might be enough so we can salvage something from 'bout the worst season we ever lived through."

"I don't know what your game is, Slocum, but I don't like it." The banker glowered at Slocum.

"No reason for you to like anything about me, Harlow, because there's nothing about you I like."

Slocum moved with blinding speed, shifting his aim from the banker's head to the far gunman. He had let his horse edge away just enough so that he thought his actions were hidden by his partner as he went for his six-gun. Slocum's round caught the man in the chest, knocking him off his horse. The horse reared in fright and kicked out, disturbing the second gunman's chance to go for his smoke wagon.

Slocum saw the man was more occupied with staying in the saddle of his rearing horse than fighting. He swung his Colt back to the banker, who was going for the pistol he carried in his shoulder holster.

Slocum smiled. The banker blanched at the sight and slowly took his hand away from the butt of his pistol. He had looked in the face of death and knew he was lucky to have slipped away alive.

"Get out of here and don't bother the Newcombes again anytime soon," Slocum said.

Harlow and his unwounded assistant helped get the third man on his horse. Slocum saw that his slug had only grazed the man's ribs, but the wound probably hurt like hellfire. He watched as the trio rode slowly away, almost reaching the distant road before Slocum holstered his six-gun.

"You've made yourself a powerful enemy," Mrs. Newcombe said. "He won't let you get by with shamin' him the way you did."

"What's life without an enemy or two?" Slocum touched the brim of his dusty Stetson and started to leave.

"Wait!" called Newcombe. "You didn't have to do that. Any of that. You saved our farm."

Slocum said nothing. He had probably saved their lives.

"Please, come on in and have some dinner. Isn't much but it'll go a ways toward payin' you back." Newcombe held up the receipt Slocum had forced Harlow to write to show what he meant, as if Slocum might have forgotten already. The offer wasn't one Slocum could turn down.

"That's mighty kind of you. I'm not all that hungry, having eaten not too long ago, but a glass of water would go down good."

"I . . . I have some peach pie," Mrs. Newcombe said almost shyly.

"We got the peaches from a Navajo passing through. Claimed they were from new peach trees down in the Canyon de Chelly. They might be, but they're dried peaches. Does that matter, Mr. Slocum?"

"Not at all," Slocum said, handing the reins of his Appaloosa to the wide-eyed silent urchin standing beside him. They went into the cool, dim interior of the house. Slocum had eaten better peach pie but none so earnestly given to him.

11

"You want another, Slocum?" asked the barkeep. Benjamin reached under the bar and pulled out a whiskey bottle with a label on it. This caught Slocum's attention. Most of the tarantula juice served here came in plain bottles, obviously the "house" brand.

"Real rye?" Slocum asked.

"Actual stuff, all the way from Tennessee," the barkeep assured him.

"Why are you offering it?"

"I heard what you did out there." Benjamin jerked his thumb over his shoulder in the direction of the Newcombe place. "I'm good friends with 'em, and they deserve better than Harlow is dishing out." The bartender poured a shot with great deliberation, as if spilling a single drop would doom him forever to hell. He carefully pushed it across the bar.

Slocum picked up the shot glass and took a whiff of the aroma rising like mist after a gentle rain. This wasn't the usual trade whiskey colored with gunpowder and rusty nails.

"Much obliged," Slocum said, starting to drink. The

glass suddenly flew from his hand, sailing across the room to shatter against the wall.

Slocum spun, only to have a heavy hand push him back. His hand made it halfway to the butt of his six-shooter before he stopped. Eustace Harlow held him by the throat with his left hand and in his right was the small caliber pistol usually slung under his arm.

"I ought to kill you where you stand, Slocum. How dare you interfere with a business transaction!"

Slocum considered his chances. Bent back over the bar the way he was, with Harlow's hand clenched on his throat, he wasn't able to get out of the way fast enough to survive. The banker had his pistol cocked and pointed at Slocum's face. Dodging a bullet or clearing leather with his own piece wasn't likely.

"You spilled my drink," Slocum said.

"What?" This took Harlow aback. It was not the reaction he had expected.

In that instant of surprise, Slocum moved, bringing his hand up to the one gripping his throat. He twisted slightly against the banker's fingers to loosen the hold, pried away the choking fingers, then jerked hard on Harlow's thumb. The man yelped in pain and swung his pistol off-target.

Slocum came erect, then applied pressure on the captive hand, forcing Harlow to his knees.

"Drop the gun," Slocum said. "Drop it now."

A man used to roughhousing would have blown Slocum's belly out with a single shot and devil take the hindmost. The pain was too much for Harlow, and he did as he was ordered.

Slocum didn't release his hold but looked up. The two bullyboys who had been with Harlow at the Newcombe place stood with their six-shooters trained on him. The one he had shot looked as if his face had turned to chalk, but the six-gun in his hand was steady.

"He's going to buy me another drink since he spilled my first one," Slocum said, twisting his grip a little more and sending lances of pain all the way up to Harlow's shoulder.

"Let the boss go," said the pale, wounded gunman.

"Or you'll shoot me in cold blood?"

"It'd be my privilege," said the gunman. Slocum saw the man's finger tightening on the trigger.

"Do it and there'll be two pieces of you to bury. This here scattergun's loaded with carpet tacks." Benjamin had reached under the bar and pulled out a sawed-off shotgun. He rested it on the bar, pointed in the gunman's direction.

"Quite a dilemma," Slocum said. "Die or do the sensible thing."

"Do it, do it," grated out Harlow when Slocum turned his wrist a bit more.

"For once, your boss has a good idea," Benjamin said.

The gunman reluctantly lowered the hammer on his six-gun and shoved it back into his holster. The other one followed suit, but Slocum saw how he was thinking how he could get off a shot at the barkeep, then Slocum. And he didn't much care if the banker was hit in the process. Slocum had seen this one's like before. Killing was pleasurable to him.

Eustace Harlow had hired himself a pair of sidewinders, capable of killing without giving any warning.

"How much did that bottle of rye cost?" Slocum asked over his shoulder, keeping his punishing grip on the banker's hand.

"Twenty dollars. Shipped all the way from Tennessee, like I told you."

"Then thank Mr. Harlow for buying us each a bottle of it. That's forty dollars, Harlow." Slocum bent forward slightly, putting his weight into the grip. He felt bones beginning to yield in the man's trapped hand.

"Ge-get my wallet. Inside pocket."

Slocum plucked the wallet free and tossed it onto the bar.

"Take what you need. And be sure to take enough to replace the broken shot glass."

"This is robbery!" grated out Harlow.

"Such a nice shot glass probably cost at least ten dollars. Wouldn't you say so, Benjamin?"

"Yep, Slocum, that I would." The barkeep was enjoying this, but Slocum knew it was only a matter of seconds before the two gunmen decided to ignore their boss and the cushy jobs he had given them and start shooting.

He released the banker. As he did so, he stepped back so he could throw down on the gunmen if they showed the slightest inclination of carrying on the feud. He had read them right. Both looked disappointed that they weren't going to kill anyone that day.

"Why don't you gents step outside?" suggested Benjamin. "Just so's me and the banker can finish our transaction." The barkeep thumbed through the sheaf of currency in Harlow's wallet, took fifty out and tossed the wallet with the remainder of the money onto the sawdust-covered floor. "Thank you kindly, Mr. Harlow. I appreciate a man who pays what he owes."

Slocum was glad to see that Benjamin wasn't inclined to rub salt into the wounds. The indignity Harlow had already suffered might be enough reason for him to resort to backshooting. Any further disgrace would guarantee it.

"You'll pay for this, Slocum. I swear," Harlow said, scrambling along like a crab before getting to his feet.

"Foreclose on my loan," Slocum said. "I'll be waiting." He knew he'd have to watch his back while he was in Dehydration, especially if he didn't see either of Harlow's henchmen in front of him.

Suddenly, Benjamin went up on tiptoe to peer past the banker. "What's the fuss about outside?"

"Mr. Harlow, there's a fire!" shouted the gunman Slocum had wounded out at the Newcombe farm. "We kin see the flames leapin' way up into the sky!"

Slocum grabbed the barkeep by the arm and swung him around. The man was heading for the door to go look.

"Make sure you've got anything that'll burn—all your whiskey—where it'll be safe," Slocum said. "Bury it if you can." He didn't want to tell Benjamin that he wanted the whiskey out of the way so it wouldn't feed the fire. Alcohol could ignite the tinder-dry town as if dynamite had been planted under it.

"Good idea, Slocum. You got quite a head for business on your shoulders. You ever think about buyin' into a saloon?"

"Tend to the whiskey," Slocum said, following the banker into the street. The rest of the town had already gathered. Slocum smelled the smoke the instant he stepped outside the saloon, but it took him a few seconds to realize that no buildings in town were on fire. The flames danced along the horizon, out on the prairie. As dry as it was, fire could wipe out half of Wyoming before burning itself out.

"That's out in the direction of the Newcombes," Pete Tahlmann said, squinting. "There's not a whole lot between them and the town, and the wind's comin' this way."

Slocum almost choked on the dense smoke now. If the wind kicked up any more, it would blow the fire down main street.

"Is there any gully or deep ravine between here and there?" asked Slocum. His mind raced. There wasn't any water to put out the fire, and it had already grown to such a conflagration that they could not form a fire line and beat it out with blankets or just throw dirt on it.

"The riverbed," Tahlmann said. "But the Sulphur River's all dammed up, Slocum. The bed's as dry as the prairie itself."

"The riverbed," Slocum said. "We've got to use it as a

firebreak. That's the only way we're going to save the town."

"Do it, do as he says!" shrieked Eustace Harlow. "You can't let the whole damned town go up in smoke!"

Slocum knew the banker's concern was less for the people in Dehydration than it was for the buildings, most of which were probably mortgaged to the hilt through his bank.

"Get shovels from Tahlmann's store," Slocum shouted. "Clear all the brush along the riverbanks. Keep the fire from catching on this side of the river!"

There was a wild scramble for tools followed by a rush to the bank of the dry river. Slocum used a rake to pull away the dead plants men with picks and shovels uprooted. As he worked he felt the heat of the fire on his face, blistering him. This spurred him on to work harder. As he dragged the piles of dried vegetation back out of the path of the fire, he couldn't help but think how easy it would be for Trent Campbell to break the dam and let the Sulphur River return to its proper course. The rush of water would insure that Dehydration wasn't burned into a cinder.

But the minutes dragged into an hour, and the river remained as dry as it had been when he had first ridden into town. It was impossible that Campbell didn't know about the prairie fire. He had guards posted up high along the canyon walls. So much smoke and the towering flames had to be visible from miles off. From the aerie of the Circle C sentries, they had to be wondering about friends in town.

After this fire, they wouldn't have any friends.

"Dang, Slocum, the fire keeps comin'," complained Tahlmann. Slocum hardly recognized the man. His face was coated with soot broken only by the rivulets of sweat washing away the blackness.

"We're stopping it, though," Slocum answered. "The fire's got to run out of dried bushes on the other side sometime."

"Mighty long stretch of river we have to scrape clear," Tahlmann said. "But we're doing it. Nobody's hanging back. The whole town's pitchin' in!"

Slocum looked around and saw that the storekeeper was almost right. Eustace Harlow and his gunmen were nowhere to be seen, but not a dozen yards away Mrs. Jenkins struggled to carry buckets of water from town to the struggling firemen, not to throw on the flames but for the thirsty men to drink. And beyond her Maddy Villareal worked with a hoe, cutting dried grama off at the ground and pulling it away to rob the fire of its fodder.

Slocum made his way toward the spot where Maddy worked so diligently.

"How're you doing?" he asked. The roar of the fire was dying down as it moved away, but a shift in the wind would endanger the town and all its citizens again.

"This is as hard as I've worked in years," she said, grinning. Her white teeth shone through the mask of soot on her face. Slocum bent over and kissed her. She recoiled, eyes wide. "Why, John. I am surprised."

"Don't be. I'll show you real fire when we're finished here."

"Let me fan myself," she said, making waving motions with her hand.

"Slocum, Slocum!" came the shout, reaching across the entire fire line.

"Stay out of trouble," Maddy chided. "Oh, never mind. Trouble finds you." She threw her arms around his neck and gave him a real kiss, not the little peck he had given her. She pushed away, sighed heavily and went back to scraping the ground with her hoe.

"Slocum, where the deuce are you?"

Slocum retraced his steps and found the barkeep looking around frantically.

"What is it, Benjamin?"

"God, there you are, Slocum. The Newcombes! They

were trapped out on the prairie. We've got to go rescue them."

Slocum stared into the sheets of flame licking at the sky on the far side of the dry riverbed and shook his head. There was no way anyone could get out to the Newcombe farm alive. And if someone did, the chance of finding any of them alive was close to zero.

"It don't look good, I know, Slocum, but you got to try. We'll go. You and me. The two of us!"

Slocum looked at Benjamin more closely. The barkeep had stuck up for him when Harlow and his two henchmen had tried to gun him down, but still, he hadn't expected such charity—or bravery.

"We can't make it. Too much fire. The smoke."

"We can tie damp rags over our horses' noses. Same for us. If you won't go, I'll have to try it by myself."

"Why? What's so important about the Newcombe family?"

"Sarah's my sister. She's all the family I got left. And those two little girls. They're my nieces."

"Stay here," Slocum said. "I'll do what I can."

"I can help."

"You'll be in the way. Taking care of myself's going to be a chore. I don't want to have to play wet nurse to you, too." Slocum saw that the harsh words didn't offend Benjamin. If anything, the relief on the man's face told the real story. Still, Slocum knew Benjamin would have tried to reach his sister's family if he hadn't volunteered.

He ran to the stables and got the rags needed to keep his horse from keeling over under him from the smoke. The Appaloosa didn't take kindly to having the wet rag put over his nose, but Slocum persevered, then soaked his own bandanna and wrapped it around his face. He made sure he had a canteen filled with water, though the small amount would hardly matter.

Before mounting, he plunged himself into a water barrel

all the way to the waist. Soaking wet, he rode hard out of town. He waved to Benjamin as he galloped past and sent his horse directly for the river. Hooves kicking up charred plants and occasional sparks, the Appaloosa plunged on. Slocum burst through the curtain of flame on the far side of the river and entered a world so totally alien that he hardly recognized it.

The prairie had been charred as far as he could see. Only the sheets of flame gnawing at the riverbank remained, but in the far distance he saw wisps of smoke rising, telling him that the fire had already raced eastward with gut-wrenching speed. That meant it had already swept over the Newcombe farm.

He slowed his pace and finally let the horse walk to regain its wind. The choking odors rising were as much from burnt flesh as it was from charred plants. Only burrowing animals had survived, and not many of them.

He rode directly to the Newcombe house—or where it had been. The smoldering walls were all that remained. The roof had collapsed. The barn was gone. Anyone in either of the structures had to have died since there was nowhere to hide, nowhere to run.

Slocum dismounted and poked through the ruins, hunting for bodies. Benjamin would want to give them a Christian burial. But Slocum didn't see any sign of the family.

He froze when he heard a scratching sound. He looked around and saw nothing living, unless the distant hungry fire could be considered a thing alive. Slocum thought he was hearing things, but the scratching was replaced with a pounding he could not dismiss. He began digging through the rubble at the rear of the house and uncovered a cellar door.

"Help!" came the faint cry from inside.

"I'll get you out in two shakes of a lamb's tail," he said, struggling to move the last of the debris away. With the survivors inside pushing and Slocum pulling, the door soon popped open.

A grateful Newcombe, his wife and two children rushed out.

"You came for us," Mrs. Newcombe said in awe.

"Wanted more of that fine peach pie," Slocum said. "Benjamin tried to come out but he was caught up saving Dehydration from the fire."

"It got that far?" asked Newcombe. "I figured they only intended to burn us out. I didn't think they'd try to burn the whole damn town."

"Who?" demanded Slocum. "Who tried to burn you out?"

As much as he hated to admit it, Slocum didn't believe what Newcombe told him.

12

Slocum stood at the rear of the saloon as most of the town crowded in to hear what Newcombe had to say.

"The fire was set," Newcombe said. "I saw riders out 'bout where the fire blazed up. And they was Harlow's henchmen."

"The banker tried to burn you out? Why?"

"He tried to buy my place but Slocum there helped out, so he couldn't drive me out. Harlow wants the land something fierce, but he didn't need my house or barn. Or my family."

Slocum watched Benjamin's reaction. It was about what he expected. The barkeep turned red in the face and reached for the shotgun under the bar. Before he could drag it out and demand everyone go lynch Harlow, Slocum spoke up.

"That's well and good but those two owlhoots have three witnesses that they were nowhere near your farm."

"What's that? Who? Who'd vouch for them varmints?" demanded Tahlmann. The storekeeper had blood in his eye. Slocum knew the merchant thought of this as his town and he aimed to protect it.

"Me. I saw them when the fire started. Harlow, too."

Silence fell, then an ugly murmur grew. Slocum caught the drift of the whispered words. They wondered why he was in cahoots with somebody who'd start a fire.

"You said there was another witness. Who?"

"Him. Benjamin was here when the three of them tried to rough me up. I had a grip on Harlow and my gun trained on the other two. They'd just been thrown out—by Benjamin—when the cry of fire went up. Isn't that true, Benjamin?"

"Well, yeah, what you say is so. They were in here when the fire was spotted. Then Slocum warned me to be sure my whiskey was safe and secure, so it wouldn't blow up the rest of the town."

"When you got outside, Harlow was yelping like a scalded dog about somebody putting out the fire. His two henchmen were with him," Slocum said.

"That's right," Benjamin agreed reluctantly.

The crowd grumbled a bit more but subsided. They might not take Slocum's word, but they had to believe Benjamin. It was his sister and her family that had been at risk. If anyone wanted to bring the right men to justice, it was the barkeep.

"So who did it?" asked Newcombe.

"What can you tell us about the men you saw? Were they from the Bar None?" demanded Tahlmann.

"Didn't recognize them as being from there. Chet and a few of his boys stop by now and again. Real friendly fellows. They even help out when they can. I didn't recognize any of them as being Bar None outriders."

"Might have been them worthless Injuns what danced and hooted and hollered," someone at the far side of the saloon said.

"They weren't Arapaho. I know them by sight. You remember how we all stood together against their raidin' parties?" asked Newcombe. "I won't forget they way they look, not any time soon. These was white men. Cowboys."

"What else do you remember about them?" asked Tahlmann. "There's got to be something."

"I saw a flash from one of them's hat. Like they wore a hatband with silver concha on it. You know, like a Mexican vaquero might wear."

Slocum jerked around when Maddy gasped. She put her hand to her mouth, then backed away and slipped out the back door. Slocum hesitated, then followed in time to see Maddy running as hard as she could for the edge of town. He wondered if she was returning to the boardinghouse— or had some other destination in mind. He quickly found out.

She veered away from Mrs. Jenkins's and kept running, stumbling now and out of breath, toward the road leading west into the mountains.

Slocum stopped some distance away when Maddy began shouting at empty air. He thought she had gone off her rocker, then saw movement from farther along the road. Someone had been sitting in the shade of a tall, spindly pine.

Marsh Campbell.

Slocum's hand went toward his six-shooter, but the range was too great. Worse than not being able to shoot the man, Slocum was too far away to hear what Maddy was saying. Her arms flew about wildly, and she was decidedly agitated. When she reached up and grabbed Marsh's hat, Slocum caught the glint of silver from the headband. He couldn't tell what caused the flash of light, but it might be a Mexican concha.

Like the one Newcombe had said he saw on the rider who had set the fire.

Slocum marched directly toward them, but neither caught sight of him. When he got within twenty yards, Marsh turned and bolted, leaving Maddy still yelling at him.

Slocum added his voice to the woman's.

"Stop, stop or I'll shoot you down!" he called. Marsh

ran faster. By the time Slocum reached Maddy's side, only the echo of a galloping horse remained to show that Marsh Campbell had ever been there.

"He didn't do it, John. I swear, he didn't do it. Marsh wouldn't start a fire like that."

Slocum stared at her. Maddy was adamant. And her protests carried the ring of truth to them. Slocum hadn't gotten to know Marsh Campbell at all. The man had been half dead when Slocum had turned him over to his father, but more than sincerity in the woman's voice worried at Slocum's condemnation of Marsh for the crime.

"He wasn't even out on the range, was he? Where was he hiding?"

"Here. I was talking to him when the alarm went up."

"Could it have been somebody else from the Circle C who set the fire?"

"Trent Campbell is a son of a bitch, but he had no reason to set a fire," Maddy said, her heat matching that of the prairie fire.

"Who set the fire, then?"

"Maybe no one. It's dry, John. Or hadn't you noticed? Any kind of a spark could have set the whole state on fire. Dry lightning?"

"No clouds," Slocum pointed out. But he knew she was right. Any number of other things could account for the fire. A carelessly left campfire from someone passing through. He had seen haystacks spontaneously combust for no good reason. And any spark might have ignited the blaze that had almost destroyed Dehydration and killed the Newcombe family.

"He didn't do it," she said adamantly.

"Newcombe saw someone with a silver concha on his hatband. Like Marsh was wearing."

"But he couldn't identify Marsh," she said.

"Calm down. I don't know why I should, but I believe you."

"Thanks," Maddy said tartly. "You think I'd lie about being with him when the fire started?"

"No, because that'd mean you two were in cahoots if he started it."

The woman's dark eyes widened in shock, and she tried to speak. No words came out.

"I said I believe you, but they might not." Slocum saw the dozen or more mounted men coming up the road. He knew a lynch mob when he saw one, and this was certainly an angry one.

"Benjamin remembered how fond of silver concha Marsh Campbell was. We're goin' up to have a word with him." The grizzled old codger Gus led the posse. Slocum saw some defectors from the lynch mob.

"Where's Pete Tahlmann?" he asked. "Does he have too much sense to waste his time? Or Benjamin or Newcombe?"

"They're back at the saloon. Ain't got no reason to involve them. They been through enough."

"Does Pete Tahlmann even know you're taking the law into your own hands?" asked Slocum.

"Screw Pete Tahlmann," growled Gus. "He don't tell us what to do. He's got no spine when it comes to lawbreakers. All we're gonna do is ask Marsh Campbell real polite-like if he is still wearin' a hat with a Meskin concha on it."

"And if he is, what's that prove?"

"Reckon we've found ourselves a firebug."

"It doesn't mean somebody else didn't set the fire," Slocum said, but he saw logic meant nothing. The men were angry and wanted to take it out on somebody. Since Harlow and his men weren't likely targets, they had to move father afield. All the way up the canyon to the Circle C and Marsh Campbell.

"I—" began Maddy. Slocum silenced her. Nothing she said would amount to a hill of beans convincing these men. They rode past, leaving her standing in the dust.

"John, you said you believed me. You saved Marsh before. You can't let them lynch him for something he didn't do!"

"He's safe enough as long as he stays on the Circle C." Slocum looked at her closely. "He'll stay there, won't he?"

"He can't be made a prisoner on his own land, John."

"Seems the folks would be more inclined to put away their nooses if that dam was blown up." Slocum saw Maddy struggling with some dilemma but didn't stay to hear what she might say. She was right about one thing. He ought to ride along to make sure nobody got into too much trouble. Slocum remembered his brief excursion into Circle C land and the gunfire he had drawn.

Slocum took his Appaloosa from the stall, saddled it and then rode at a steady clip after the posse. When he passed the spot where Maddy had spoken to Marsh Campbell the woman was gone. He hoped she had returned to the boardinghouse and would stay out of trouble, but that hardly seemed likely considering how headstrong she was.

Slocum wondered that Campbell's sentries let the posse get as far into the canyon as they had. The dam was within gunshot. So were a half-dozen armed hands from the Circle C. Slocum looked to the canyon rim but didn't see any gunmen up there. Trent Campbell might have brought them down to reinforce the tight knot of guards on the dam.

"We want Marsh Campbell!" Gus shouted. "Send the varmint out!"

"What do you want my boy for?" Trent Campbell's voice blared like a lion's roar. The man stood on the top of the dam, a rifle resting in the crook of his arm.

"He set the prairie fire that damned near killed us all! Send him out so he can stand trial."

Trent Campbell laughed harshly. Even at this distance Slocum could see the man shaking his head, as if deciding whether to suffer these fools any longer. The rancher was at the edge of losing his temper. If he did he had a half-dozen riflemen to back him up. They had the advantage of height, probably had redoubts built and were already keyed up. One or two bullets sailing through the middle of the posse would scatter them.

"Go home. There's nothing for you here," Campbell bellowed.

"We want Marsh. He's a criminal. We can't let 'im go unpunished."

"Marsh has been up here with me. He wasn't anywhere near that fire."

Slocum tensed. He knew that was a lie. He believed Maddy when she said Marsh had been with her. There was no reason for her to say he had been in Dehydration if he had really been on the Circle C land, and she wanted to protect him. Being on the far side of the dam was a better alibi than being with her.

"We want to talk to him, Campbell. Send him on down or we're comin' up."

"I don't tolerate trespassing," Trent Campbell shouted.

"You cut off our damn water!" someone shouted. "Let us have our river back!"

Slocum knew this was closer to the reason for the townspeople's anger than anything Marsh Campbell might have done, even setting fire to the prairie. And it was more likely to be the spark that set off another fire that would end in deaths.

"Let's tear down that dam," another grumbled. "Ain't gonna be a town much longer without our water."

"You whined about the floods," Campbell called down from the top of the dam. "You wanted something done when the Sulphur River flooded you out year after year, so I spent my own money to build this dam."

"Didn't think you'd steal all our water."

"I saved *my* town more 'n once," Campbell said. "This here dam's saved the town from spring floods and now it's saving the Circle C."

"It's not all your water. We deserve some of it. Enough to survive!"

Slocum wasn't sure who shot first. It was probably someone from Dehydration, but he couldn't swear to it. The bullets began flying in both directions so fast that he hardly had time to wheel his horse around and hightail it back down the canyon. The guards usually posted along the rim must have been pulled back to protect the dam when the posse was spotted because Slocum saw no hint anyone waited above him.

He reined in and stopped. It sounded like Gettysburg back at the foot of the dam—and was likely to turn into Antietam, with blood flowing down the dried river all the way to Dehydration. Slocum saw no way he could pry the posse loose, but he might get Campbell to stop shooting long enough to let those who had survived to escape. Heaving a deep sigh, he swung his Appaloosa back toward the dam and advanced at a cautious walk.

"Campbell!" Slocum shouted, his voice booming, echoing, carrying to the Circle C owner. "Let them go. If they put down their guns, let them go!"

The next furious fusillade died with only one or two shots following.

"Why'd I want to do a fool thing like that?"

"Why do you want to murder them?"

"They're trying to steal my water!"

"It's our water," someone cut in. A few more bullets whined off rocks, silencing the man. Slocum hoped there wouldn't be any more debate on the point. Campbell held all the aces.

"They're backing away now," Slocum called. He rode forward to a bend in the canyon so he could see that the posse was obeying. Their rage had changed to fear for their lives. Slocum doubted any of the men would learn anything from this fight, but he hoped one or two might think twice before they tried a suicidal frontal assault like this again.

By ones and twos they retreated. Slocum couldn't remember how many had been in the posse but thought all had survived. Whether Campbell's cowboys were lousy marksmen or simply didn't care to kill any of the men who had been their neighbors hardly mattered. A few in the posse carried minor wounds but nothing that would cause them to bleed to death before they got back to town.

"Thanks," Slocum shouted.

"Go to hell. All of you!" Campbell returned.

Slocum reached out and grabbed Gus's arm to keep him from lifting his six-shooter and taking a futile shot at the rancher.

"Don't provoke him. They hold the high ground and have us boxed in. There'll be another day to fight."

Gus grumbled and jerked away, trotting off. Slocum followed the posse at a distance, not wanting to look as if he had aligned himself with the hotheads.

As he rode out of the canyon mouth, he chanced to look up. A flash of light shone off something silver. Slocum fished his field glasses out of his saddlebags and slowly panned along the rim until he found the source of the reflection.

Marsh Campbell.

Campbell was looking through binoculars of his own toward town. Whatever he stared at completely held his attention. He didn't bother turning his glasses to the posse once. Slocum swung his pair to the backs of the posse, then away from them toward Mrs. Jenkins's boardinghouse.

Madelaine Villareal stood outside, waving to Marsh Campbell.

13

Slocum let the posse go to the saloon to drown their sorrows and to breast-beat, telling one another how it would have been different, if only . . .

He rode directly for the boardinghouse and dismounted. Maddy was nowhere to be seen. Looking over his shoulder toward the distant canyon rim, Slocum no longer saw any hint that Marsh Campbell stood there, watching. Watching and waiting. That was the part Slocum wanted to find out about. What was the son of the Circle C owner waiting for and what did Maddy have to do with it?

Slocum walked up to the front door but didn't knock. He saw Maddy in a small stand of trees some distance away, sitting on a stump, face in her hands. Slocum went to her. She never heard him until he was within arm's length. Then she jerked upright and stared at him with wide, dark eyes. He couldn't tell if she had been crying, but she might have been.

"Tell me about it," he said.

"Tell you what?"

"Don't play dumb," he said, holding down his anger. "What's going on between you and Marsh Campbell? I saw him watching you through field glasses, and I saw you waving back."

"He's such an annoying man," she said, more than a hint of bitterness in her words. "I wish he would go away."

"How far away?"

"He keeps annoying me," she said.

"Here," Slocum said, pulling out a small derringer from a vest pocket. He handed it to her.

"Wh-what am I supposed to do with this?"

"Shoot the son of a bitch when he annoys you again," Slocum said.

"I don't know anything about guns. I'd be more of a danger to myself than to him." She held it out to him to take back.

"I'll show you how to use it."

She looked up at him, her midnight eyes fixed on him. She smiled just a little, turned away and then glanced at him over her shoulder, averting her eyes slightly. Then she locked his gaze and challenged him boldly.

"Show me," she said. Maddy walked away into the wooded area, her backside swaying from side to side enough to distract Slocum. He tucked the derringer away and went after her, wondering if he was reading her right.

He was.

Slocum caught up with her just as she turned and threw her arms out. She clung to his neck and pulled their bodies together hard and their lips even harder. The kiss set Slocum's pulse pounding. Maddy's hand roved the back of his head, lacing through his hair, keeping him from moving away—as if he would. Their lips parted just enough, and Slocum was not surprised to find they both had the same erotic idea.

Their tongues collided, slid past one another and then began a game of hide and seek that excited both of them. Maddy's tongue darted about, lightly touching, caressing, vanishing to entice him to explore her mouth. Back and forth they moved, bodies and mouths striving.

Slocum's hands roved over the willing woman's back, then slid lower so he could cup her round, firm buttocks. He pulled her even closer. He felt her breasts crushing beneath her blouse against his chest. Her nipples hardened and threatened to poke holes in him. He wanted more.

He broke off the kiss and looked at her. Maddy's eyes were half-closed, her ruby lips slightly parted and everything about her, even the wild disarray of her raven-black hair, was delightful, delectable, desirable.

Moving slowly, he kissed her cheeks and eyes, then moved to her ears. She turned her head this way and that to let him lavish his kisses. As he did so, Slocum felt her hands moving slowly downward, around and to the buttons holding his fly.

"Let me—" he started.

"No! I want to do it. In my own time." Maddy threw her head back to get a lock of hair out of her eyes. Her long black mane caught on the vagrant wind like a lazy garrison pennant.

Slocum let her work methodically on getting his fly open. Then she discarded his gun belt. He was breathing hard by the time her hand curled around him and squeezed gently.

"So warm and hard."

"All yours," Slocum said.

"I know. And I want every inch of it." Maddy dropped to her knees and took him in her mouth. A lance of pure delight jolted Slocum and forced him to lean back against a tree. Her avid mouth worked up and down his rigidity with licking and tonguing and delicate kisses that sent his pulse racing wildly.

He looked down and saw only the top of her head as she burrowed into his crotch. But he felt her every movement.

How he felt her mouth! Hot breath gusted around him and tickled to the point that he was as aroused by this as he was by her tonguing. He rested his hands on her head and guided her back and forth in a motion that caused his knees to buckle. He started sliding down the tree trunk so that the bark cut and tore at his back.

When he was seated on the ground, legs stretched out, Maddy came up for air. The beautiful woman's eyes were wild with lust. Her chest heaved and begged Slocum for attention. He reached out and grabbed a double handful of cloth. With a powerful jerk, he sent her buttons sailing out onto the fragrant carpet of pine needles.

Her naked brown breasts glowed in the soft light filtering through the pines. Slocum bent forward, cupped one and then began suckling. It was Maddy's turn to moan and sigh in pleasure. He worked on the left and then transferred his oral attentions to the right. Next he ran his hands around her slender waist and drew her closer.

A leg flashed in the sunlight as Maddy straddled his waist. She settled down so he could continue exploring every inch of her flesh with his tongue and lips. He was as thorough with her breasts as she had been with his hardened manhood.

"More, I need more," she said, leaning forward and lifting her hips off his lap so she could whisper in his ear. "Give it to me. I know you are ready."

Slocum reached under the woman's skirts and got the unwanted cloth pushed up around her waist. His hands stroked over bare thighs and worked around to the crinkly nest hidden between her legs.

"You're not wearing anything under those skirts," he accused.

"Just for you, John, for you, my darling!"

A part of Slocum knew this was a lie but another part knew it did not matter. He ran his hand up and down between her legs, feeling her arousal, savoring the heat building within her core. She reached up and grabbed a tiny limb on the tree to give herself stability as Slocum maneuvered his hardness beneath her nether lips.

"Now," he whispered hoarsely. Then Slocum cried out as she plunged down, ramming him into her tender tunnel with great force.

Slocum stroked beneath her skirt, along her thighs and around to the fleshy mounds of her delicious rump. He squeezed and kneaded those two half moons until Maddy was sobbing with need. But he held her in place, not letting her move. He was hidden entirely within her tightness. The heat and moisture seeped around his fleshy plug and into him, drilling down all the way into his loins.

"Move, move, please, this is killing me," Maddy whimpered. Her entire body shook like an earthquake was building. Slocum held her firmly. The delights within his own body were too intense for him to ever want her to move.

But nature required motion. She pushed herself up a little on her knees, letting him slide out of her interior with a slick pop! Before either could say a word, Maddy simply relaxed. Her hips fell and he slid within her again.

This time she began a slow circular motion that was sweet torture for both of them. But Slocum was reaching the limits of his endurance. He reached out and gripped each of her cherry-hard nubbins, cresting her breasts between thumb and forefinger, and squeezed rhythmically. This drove Maddy wild.

She rose and fell on him as he released and squeezed down with his fingers. She moved faster; he squeezed faster. She moved slower; Slocum bent over and kissed those luscious melons. But they were both approaching the limit of their desire.

As Maddy cried out in release, Slocum spilled his seed. He reached around her body and held her close, his hips rising off the ground under her weight in an attempt to probe deeper. She crammed herself down hard to take more of him. But soon the ecstasy began to fade, and they slumped against each other, drained.

"Oh, John, that was so good," she said softly.

"It was," he agreed. She rocked back and looked at him through slightly glazed eyes. He kissed her, trying to remember what he had wanted to ask her before they had embarked on this delicious tryst.

"The fire," he said suddenly.

"What about it?"

Slocum still struggled to remember what he had wanted to ask Maddy, but it was gone from his brain. Replacing what he wanted from her was a new question.

"Who else was out on the prairie when the fire started?"

"It wasn't Marsh!"

He lifted her up. Maddy struggled to her knees, then got to her feet and tried to smooth her wrinkled skirts. She looked around and began picking up the buttons that had popped free of her blouse when Slocum's passions had flared.

"No, it wasn't." Slocum remembered what he had wanted to ask Maddy before she had seduced him, but it hardly seemed as important now. She had distracted him well, but there was no call for her to go to such lengths. Slocum was glad they had stolen this moment, but he didn't need her lovemaking to make him believe that she had been with Marsh when the fire started.

Slocum got to his feet, picking up his gun belt and swinging it around his waist.

Maddy looked up from her hunt for her buttons, then smiled.

"*You* need to be buttoned up." She came to him on her knees and tucked him into his jeans, then quickly buttoned his fly. "You ought to be glad I didn't treat your buttons like you did mine."

"You liked it," Slocum said.

"I loved it," Maddy said, as if this had only just occurred to her. "I needed it. Thank you, John."

"Is Newcombe still in town?"

"At the saloon, I'd suspect," she said. But Slocum was already on his way to Benjamin's gin mill, his mind going over what he knew and what he suspected.

Slocum swung through the double doors into the saloon.

Benjamin and Newcombe sat at a table to the side of the bar, a bottle between them. The way the barkeep looked at Slocum confirmed what he suspected. The bartender was nobody's fool and had either guessed or heard the real story.

Dragging over a chair from a nearby table, Slocum sat down facing Newcombe. The farmer's eyes were bloodshot and his hand shook.

"Fessing up will make it easier on your conscience," Slocum said.

"What? Whatya sayin'?" demanded Newcombe.

"He knows, doesn't he?" Slocum looked at Benjamin, then back to the farmer.

"He's my brother-in-law. I had to tell somebody."

"You started the fire, didn't you?"

"It was an accident. I was out tryin' to plow under some of the dead vegetation. I thought if I turned it over into the soil it might keep the dirt from blowin' away. Come next plantin' season, it'd work as fertilizer."

"What happened? Smoking?"

"My plow hit a rock. That was it. My plow hit a rock and the spark went flyin' out and I saw it and I couldn't do nuthin' 'bout it and—" Newcombe broke down crying.

Slocum felt no sympathy for the man.

"I've got no liking for Harlow and his boys, but it was wrong trying to blame them. It was worse trying to put the blame on Marsh Campbell," Slocum said.

"I saw that fancy silver concha of his a while back. It was all I could think to say."

"The posse might have caught him and strung him up," Slocum said. "You'd have an innocent man's blood on your hands then."

"How'd you figure it out?" asked Benjamin.

"It couldn't have been Marsh. He had an alibi," Slocum said more angrily than he intended. He wondered how far that alibi with Maddy went, if they had only been talking. "I knew it wasn't Harlow because he and his two gunmen were here in the saloon."

"They're bad men, all of 'em," said Newcombe. "The banker's tryin' to steal my land, and Campbell's making it possible by cuttin' off my water."

"Tell everyone in town what happened," Slocum said.

"I can't. Th-they'll string me up." Newcombe's voice quavered with abject fear.

"I don't know if I wouldn't help them," Slocum said.

"What's that?" came a querulous voice from the door.

Slocum turned and saw Eustace Harlow's two bullyboys.

"You sayin' you set the fire, Newcombe? The boss ain't gonna like that."

"It's none of his business," Benjamin said hotly, getting to his feet.

"It's reason enough to take the land from him," said the other gunman. "He destroyed property that still belongs to the bank."

"I'm payin' the mortgage. Slocum here gave me the money for three whole months!"

"That don't matter. It's in your loan that you can't do nuthin' to destroy the property or cause it to go down in value."

"You gents might have misheard," Slocum said, standing and kicking the chair away.

"He's gonna draw!" shouted the gunman on the left, slapping leather. His partner also went for his six-shooter.

Slocum was prepared for anything. When he saw the gunman's shoulder muscles tense, he was already going for his own Colt slung in his cross-draw holster. Slocum got his iron out and fanned three quick shots into one man's chest. The gunman's six-gun discharged, the bullet ripping away the wood in front of Slocum's toes.

The other gunman was slower to drag out his six-gun since he had already caught one of Slocum's bullets earlier. This saved Slocum getting his head blown off. The gunman was stiff from where his chest had been grazed, and his shot went wide by a few inches. Slocum heard the bullet whine past like a berserk wasp. Then he fanned off the last three shots into the man's chest.

The gunman staggered back a step, turned and fell through the door, half in and half out of the saloon.

The entire gunfight had lasted less than five seconds.

"Glory be," whispered Benjamin. "I never saw two men killed like that. You're fast, Slocum, damn fast."

Slocum came out of his crouch and slid his six-shooter back into its holster. Now that the fight was over, he felt his heart begin to race. He took a couple deep breaths to slow it. Men from all over town crowded into the doorway, looking at the dead bodies and at Slocum.

"What happened?" called Tahlmann, pushing his way through the crowd to get inside.

"They throwed down on Slocum," Newcombe said. "He was only defendin' himself."

"That's so," Benjamin said, still awed. "Never seen a man shoot so quick or so straight. But both of them drew, and Slocum cut them down where they stood."

Slocum saw Eustace Harlow poke his head into the saloon. He spied his dead henchmen, shot Slocum a deadly look then shouted, "He murdered them. Nobody can outdraw those two. I want him arrested."

Slocum saw the crowd begin exchanging looks. Even Tahlmann wavered. And Slocum could do nothing about the change he saw coming because his six-shooter was empty.

14

"I demand that he stand trial!" shouted Eustace Harlow. "He gunned down my two employees. He had to have ambushed them!"

"He did no such thing," Benjamin flared up. "He—"

"Be quiet," Pete Tahlmann said. He scratched his stubbled chin and shook his head. He had failed to wash out all the soot from the fire and his graying hair was almost uniform in color. "I reckon Harlow's got a point. Since the marshal cleared out, we haven't had much law enforcing in Dehydration. Then again, with most of the people movin' on, too, there's not been a whole lot of crime."

"The fire," grumbled Gus. "Them Campbells started a fire. We ought to get a *big* posse together and go after 'em!"

"Shut your tater trap, Gus," Tahlmann said without any rancor. "We got to take things one at a time, and Harlow's right about gettin' this matter settled quick-like."

Slocum wished he had reloaded his six-shooter. The expression on the faces of everyone in the crowd was the same. They wanted to strike out at someone—anyone—because they were impotent to do anything about the drought or Campbell's dam robbing them of the Sulphur

River water. All that kept them going every day was hauling water from the reeking water hole Slocum had discovered and using Professor Leonardo's Water Extract to cleanse it of its noxious minerals. Eventually they would run out of the potent purifier and be right back where they were when Slocum rode into town.

They might not say so, but all of them knew their days were numbered and this caused immense frustration and bubbling anger. He was convenient to strike out at because he was an outsider. He wished he had more than the two-shot derringer in his vest pocket.

"You want a mouthpiece to represent you, Slocum?"

"What's going on?" Slocum demanded. "If there's no marshal and no judge, how can I be arrested or stand trial?"

"Don't need a lawman. This here bunch can be called a Vigilance Committee, with all the powers and duties of a lawman," said Tahlmann. "And I'm as qualified to be a judge as I am the town mayor, since I never did either 'fore I came to Dehydration."

"I'll be on the jury," called one man after another.

"That settles it," said Tahlmann. "Trial, here and now. And you put that bottle down, Benjamin. No drinkin' during the trial. Anybody."

Tahlmann slipped his six-gun from its holster and banged the butt a couple times on the bar.

"This here trial's in session. We got six good men and true for jurors. Slocum there's the defendant charged with gunnin' down two of Harlow's hired thugs. You gonna persecute, Harlow?"

"That's prosecute, you dimwit," snapped the banker. "Yes, I will!"

"Get to it. We ain't got all day."

As far as Slocum could tell, they had all the time in the world. The farmers watched their crops die from the drought, and the only thing citizens of Dehydration had to look forward to was packing their belongings and finding another town to live in, one with more water and fewer troubles.

"He couldn't have outdrawn and outshot those two," Harlow said.

"Why not?" Cut in Tahlmann.

"They were hired gunmen, that's why. They were professionals I hired to protect my interests."

"You really mean, to beat up and scare people into payin' yer immoral interest rates," grumbled someone behind Harlow.

"Outta order," Tahlmann snapped, rapping his pistol butt on the bar. "So you're tellin' this court no man alive could outdraw your henchmen. Is that it?"

"One, maybe, but not both of them. He caught 'em unawares and murdered them."

"You got witnesses, Slocum?"

"Me!" shouted Benjamin, giving his rendition of what had happened. "And Newcombe saw it all, too, didn't you?"

Newcombe's head bobbed up and down. He looked scared, and Slocum reckoned it was because he was deciding whether to tell how the prairie fire had started.

"You got any rebuttal witnesses to these fine fellows' eyewitness accounts?" asked Tahlmann.

"They're both stretched out on the floor, dead," Harlow said.

"Then it's up to the jury to decide," Tahlmann said.

"Kin we have a shot of whiskey when we decide?" asked one man.

"That's the usual pay," Tahlmann said.

"And the foreman gits two?" The same man looked eager.

"Up to the barkeep. What's the verdict?"

"Innocent. No reason Benjamin or Newcombe would lie." With that the jury rushed to the bar and banged on it until Benjamin poured each in turn a stiff shot of whiskey.

Tahlmann moseyed over to Slocum and smiled.

"You didn't think we was railroading you, did you?"

"It was all so some of the men could get free drinks?" Slocum had to laugh. "Where's mine? I was acquitted."

"Benjamin!" shouted Tahlmann. "Two more down here. Make it snappy. We got real work to do."

Slocum waited for the drink as he watched the banker out of the corner of his eye. Harlow fumed and fussed but didn't seem too upset otherwise over the deaths of his two men. Slocum guessed this meant Harlow didn't have to pay them for work they'd already done.

"What's it like between Harlow and Trent Campbell?" Slocum asked. "Bad blood?"

Tahlmann nodded and said, "It started as healthy competition, then it got nastier by the week. Both of 'em's competitive sorts, if you know what I mean."

Slocum did. Harlow wanted to own the town, and Campbell had founded it. The Circle C owner felt he had bragging rights on what was now Dehydration and that he might eventually come to own it and the rest of the land nearby if he held out on supplying water.

"It was Harlow's idea to change the name of the town from Campbell, wasn't it?"

"Now that you mention it, he did come up with that idea. Didn't much care what it was changed to as long as it got changed."

"Like two bull elks charging at each other," Slocum said, more to himself than to the storekeeper.

"Both will end up too battered to mate, if this drought doesn't let up," Tahlmann said.

"The reward for bringing water to town's still good?"

"Right as rain," Tahlmann declared, laughing when he realized what he had said. "Strange how everything you say hints of water when you ain't got none."

"No way Campbell and Harlow would cooperate? Harlow is going to have bone dry land for who knows how long unless the Sulphur River is flowing again. What would it take for Campbell to uncork the stream?"

"More money than Harlow's got, that's for certain sure," Tahlmann said. Benjamin finally placed drinks in front of them and looked hesitantly at Slocum.

"You don't need to go spreadin' it around, son," Tahlmann said to the barkeep. "I figured it out a while back."

"About Newcombe?" Slocum was surprised.

"He ain't got the sense God gave a goose. Of course about Newcombe. He might have set the fire sneakin' a smoke when the missus wasn't lookin'—"

"Plow hit a rock and caused a spark," Benjamin blurted.

"That's as good a story as any," Tahlmann said. "Don't matter much now. Folks're safe and there's nothing much left to burn out there on the prairie. I doubt Newcombe's learned his lesson, but that's more a problem for his wife than anyone left in Dehydration."

"So you won't spread it around?" asked Benjamin.

"No reason to, unless that damn fool Gus tries to blame Marsh Campbell again." Tahlmann spat accurately into a gleaming brass cuspidor at the end of the bar. "That's what I think of Gus and his wild-eyed notions. If there was anybody left in this town who ought to hightail it, it's Gus Ferguson. Better get my carcass back to the store. Never can tell when someone'll want something."

Tahlmann slapped Slocum on the back and ambled off, the excitement for the afternoon finished. The rest of the men in the saloon drank happily, swapping improbable stories and outright lies until it was time for someone to go fetch more of the sulfurous water. Other than this chore, there wasn't much to do in town.

Slocum let a couple of the men buy him drinks, then slowly made his way out the door. He noticed that nobody had taken care of the two corpses yet. Flies buzzed around.

Slocum wondered if he propped them up in chairs on the boardwalk, would they dry out like corn husks? They could become sideshow attractions, with people coming to see the two mummified corpses, one on either side of the saloon door like watchmen.

He forgot such fanciful notions when he saw Maddy leaving town in a buckboard. Beside her on the driver's bench lay her case with the dowsing rod in it. She drove with eyes straight ahead, looking at nothing in her determination to go find water and collect the sizable reward.

Slocum called to her, but the noise of the wheels or her intense concentration prevented her from hearing. She drove on, but Slocum decided he ought to follow. He didn't hurry as he went to the stable and saw that his Appaloosa had its fill of water before he saddled up and rode after the woman. The dust cloud ahead in the road showed clearly where she headed. Slocum hung back far enough not to ride along in the choking dust and had plenty of time to veer off the road when he saw she was heading in the direction of the dry underground river.

She didn't return to the spot where she had begun dowsing before but rode farther to the north. Slocum wondered what she looked for to begin her actual work, but whatever it was she slowed, crept along for almost ten minutes, then came to a halt and leaped from the buckboard.

Slocum got out his field glasses and watched as she took her birch Y from its case and rubbed it slowly down each fork, as if getting a feel for its power. When she was ready, she pulled down her broad-brimmed sun hat to shade her lovely face and stepped away from the buckboard, dowsing rod in hand.

He had seen her before as she homed in on the strongest attraction. This time it took more than twenty minutes before she turned northwest and began walking slowly, as if the divining rod was pulling her along but not too powerfully.

Going to her would only break her concentration. Slocum remained on a small rise a quarter mile away, watching her progress through his binoculars. Before, she had made a beeline to the spot where they had fallen into the dry subterranean tunnel. Today she was like a broken windmill vane, flopping this way and that, never quite true and on course.

As she wandered about, the birch Y pulling her along, Slocum began surveying the prairie. Much of it was burned from Newcombe's fire but long stretches were untouched. When he spotted a wagon several miles away, he steadied himself and examined the bouncing image the best he could. Distance and heat caused a shimmer, but he eventually made out the wagon.

It was Ballantine's. The man had not left and, obviously, had not been blown up when the fire raged through this area. Slocum considered paying the man a visit to see if he had found potable water. Telling him the city supply was near, only to have it dried up, worried at Slocum's sense of honor. He hadn't known the water hole had gone dry when he told the man, nor had he known the sulfurous watering hole was the only place in the area with liquid bubbling up from the ground, but he still felt a sense of responsibility.

Before he could ride for Ballantine's camp, Slocum heard pounding hoofbeats. He swung his field glasses around and spotted a small tornado moving across the prairie, heading directly for Maddy. She seemed oblivious to the whirl of brown dust until it settled down.

Marsh Campbell called to her and caused her to lower the dowsing rod. When she saw who called out to her, her shoulders slumped and she almost dropped the birch Y. Only then did Marsh ride closer, but he never dismounted. At this distance Slocum couldn't tell what either of them said but from the way they acted, they were arguing.

Maddy began pointing, using the divining rod. She waved it about, then threw it to the ground as if in disgust.

Marsh dismounted and went to her. She backed off a pace, then stopped. Slocum saw him reach out to touch her, but she batted his hand away from her shoulder.

The argument continued, indistinct words drifting to Slocum a quarter mile off. When Maddy slapped him, Marsh jerked back. He cocked his hand as if he was going to strike her, then abruptly turned his back on her, mounted and galloped off. Maddy shouted at him as she waved her fist in the air. She stamped her foot and finally stood with her arms crossed over her chest. After venting her spleen, Maddy picked up her dowsing rod again and tried to regain the concentration she'd had before Marsh interrupted her. It was obvious she failed.

Slocum tucked his binoculars into his saddlebags and turned his horse to cut across the prairie to go after Marsh Campbell. He had failed to catch the young man before when he had taken the mountain trail and gotten to the rim of the canyon leading to the Circle C ranch.

To Slocum's exasperation, he lost him again, this time in the foothills.

15

"You're looking mighty thoughtful, Slocum," said Pete Tahlmann. The storekeeper leaned back in his chair and tilted his head slightly to study Slocum with a gimlet eye. "I've seen that look before. Mostly on men who get into big trouble. What do you have in mind?"

"Nothing much," Slocum said, jarred from his reverie. He had been staring at a spot on the saloon wall too intently for too long to appear sober, but he had only had one shot of whiskey.

"If it's so dull in Dehydration for you, we can charge you with some other trumped up crime so we can have another trial. The boys always like to get free liquor."

"One trial for murder is plenty," Slocum allowed.

"Yep, it is," Tahlmann said, but Slocum had the feeling that Tahlmann wasn't talking about bogus trials. Tahlmann smiled and continued. "The reward money's not claimed yet. As if that was a big secret." He glanced out the door. A restless wind blew dust along Dehydration's main street in proof that there was no water to be had.

"I've got an idea or two. You know what Maddy's trying, don't you?"

"Seen water witches who could waltz right on up to a

spot, let their divining rod point down and the water'd jump out of the ground." Tahlmann shook his head. "Don't know if she's foolin' herself that she has the talent or if there's no water to be found."

"Either is bad, I reckon," Slocum said. His mind still ranged far away. "She did find an underground feeder for the river."

"The Sulphur River's about as crooked as a dog's hind leg. Sometimes it's above ground, other times it burrows down like a prairie dog." Tahlmann spat and missed the cuspidor. He didn't notice because he was busy spinning his yarn. "Ever wonder what it's like bein' a prairie dog, hearin' something roarin' away just beyond your kitchen wall? So you do some digging and out comes more water than you can drink in a lifetime?"

"Lifetime's over then," Slocum said.

"Would be," Tahlmann said. "If you were a prairie dog. But the idea's the same. How do you find the right place to hear the water and dig just a mite and release it all? You have an idea on that, Slocum?"

"That reward's been on my mind," Slocum admitted.

"Nobody's gonna complain if you find a way to slake their thirst. I'd suggest you get to it. Four more families pulled up stakes and moved on."

"How'd Harlow like that?"

"Like a hungry hog at the trough. He was rooting around for their deeds before the dust settled from their wheels as they left. Won't be much longer before he owns a ghost town."

"All he has to do then is wait for the rain to come. Then he'll own not only a ready-built town but sections of prime ranch and farmland."

"Yep." Tahlmann fixed him with that piercing gaze again.

"Best get on the trail of that water," Slocum said, getting to his feet. He had a vague idea what he wanted to do. The only hitch he saw was not knowing if there was even a place to start.

After picking up supplies at Tahlmann's store, Slocum saddled his horse and rode from town. He saw that the store owner hadn't been joking about how much like a ghost town Dehydration looked. With the farming and ranching all around at an ebb, there was no commerce to support businesses in town. He had ridden through boom towns that had died when veins of gold and silver petered out and they were livelier than Dehydration.

He wanted to see if Maddy had returned from her dowsing but forced himself to ride in the opposite direction from the boardinghouse. Whatever relationship she had with Marsh Campbell was stormy. All this was something Slocum would worry about after he settled the matter of water for the town.

Using his field glasses, he located Ballantine's wagon and rode for it. He half expected to find the man dead from sunstroke but was surprised to find him sitting under the wagon bed in the shade, scribbling in a ledger.

"Slocum, my man, good to see you."

"Good to see you, too. I worried that you weren't able to find water out here."

"Water's not much concern but that fire chased me around for a spell," Ballantine said. "I've still got a few crates of dynamite left and didn't want it blown up in a prairie fire." He laughed ruefully. "Didn't want me goin' along with it, either."

"How are you staying alive with the town's watering hole all dried up?"

"What? You mean it's upped and gone dry? I was only there a couple hours ago."

"Show me."

Slocum and Ballantine went back to the water hole where Slocum had been sent originally to get water, but it was bone dry. To his surprise Ballantine kept going, past it by almost a half mile.

"I thought this was the place you told me about," Ballantine said. A small catch pocket, hardly a foot across seeped water from below. "It hardly seems enough for a town, though. Me and my horse drink the water, it takes more 'n a day to refill."

"Glad you're getting by," Slocum said, frowning as he thought. This was a poor artesian spring. If there was water beneath, drilling a deep enough well might produce water for the town. But Slocum doubted it. Water for a man and his horse, yes. But for more? There was no evidence this would ever yield more water than it had already, no matter what effort was expended.

"Any other pockets like this around?" asked Slocum.

"Nope, and I looked."

Slocum wondered why Maddy and her dowsing rod hadn't found this small dab of water. It might be she was more attuned to locating enough water for the entire town, but Slocum reckoned there was something amiss with the woman's technique.

"What do you intend to do with the dynamite you have left?" Slocum asked.

"I'm doing the calculations now," Ballantine said. "I might not be able to loft another balloon with the explosives, but there're other ways of getting it to explode in the sky and create the rain."

Ballantine waved around the ledger. Slocum saw the crabbed handwriting and the curious mathematical notations that meant nothing to him and everything to Ballantine.

"Keep at it but don't explode the bomb without my help," Slocum said.

"You'll help?" Ballantine looked at his suspiciously. "You're not gettin' a cut of the reward money. That five thousand dollars is all mine."

"I just want to be a part of history," Slocum said sardonically. This allayed Ballantine's fears.

"I'll let you know, Slocum. This is going to work like a charm. I feel it in my bones."

"In your dry bones," Slocum muttered. He pulled his horse back from the small catch pocket of water and swung into the saddle. He rode for the area where Maddy had divined the water, only to locate the empty subterranean river channel. Passing the cave-in site, he rode farther west toward the mountains until he came to the spot where he had dug like a gopher to open the ceiling of the tunnel. Slocum stared at the hole and shuddered, but he knew what he had to do.

Dismounting, he took two ropes from his saddle and secured each in a different spot, one to a rock and the other to a sturdy bush that looked as if it had put roots down to the center of the world. Slocum scrounged in his saddlebags until he got some supplies, slung them in a burlap bag over his shoulder, then took another deep breath. He had no fear of tight places, but the memory of Maddy and him being trapped came rushing back.

This time he wouldn't have her witchy powers to find the weakest spot in the roof to claw his way out if there was another cave-in.

Slocum tugged at the rope fastened around the boulder, then lowered himself into the hole. He landed on his feet, brushed away the dirt that had cascaded down around him from the quick drop, and looked farther to the west and the tunnel sloping away under the mountains.

He took out a couple of miner's candles, put one in his pocket and lit the other, putting it into a tin miner's lamp. The flickering yellow light was focused when he closed the shutter down a mite. With another deep breath to settle his nerves, he began walking. A few yards on he was bent almost double as the shaft sloped down into the bowels of the earth.

Slocum pushed forward, knowing what he looked for. Determined to find it, he even dropped to his belly and wiggled through a few tight areas. The walls turned to stone smoothed by the rush of water over the years, telling him how futile it would be to try to dig through. As he worked farther west underground, the tunnel widened so he could hardly touch both sides if he reached out, before shrinking to a tunnel so small he had to take off his gun belt to slide through. But Slocum pressed on with determination.

The candle continued to burn strongly, showing there was more than enough air, and occasionally Slocum thought he felt a breeze in his face. He stopped after a couple hours of walking and wiggling like a snake and looked up a slope of slick rock. Slick, wet rock.

Slocum snuffed out the candle and left his burlap bag, the lantern and candles behind. Working carefully up the incline, he emerged to the bright light of day.

A smile crossed his lips. He had been right about the source of the channel.

He was barely a foot above a lake stretching out for an acre or more where Trent Campbell had dammed the river. During normal weather, the Sulphur River flowed down its surface course. It also wormed its way underground through the tunnel Slocum had just traversed. As the drought had worn on, the level of the river—the artificial lake—had sunk, leaving the hole and underground tunnel high and dry.

Slocum flopped on his belly and reached down to splash water onto his face. It gave him new energy. Looking around and not seeing any of Campbell's guards, he more boldly dipped his Stetson into the lake and pulled up a full hat. He sat just inside the hole, drank deeply and looked out as he tried to figure where the guards might be.

When he had finished with the water, he put the hat back on his head and sat on the edge of the hole. Craning his neck, he looked above him and saw a ledge. Swinging up, he grabbed the rocky shelf and pulled himself to it. From here he worked all the way to the top of the dam Campbell had built across the Sulphur River.

Slocum's hand flashed for his six-shooter when he spotted a man in a red checked shirt at the far side of the dam, sitting and looking down the canyon as he smoked. The thin wisp of smoke had given him away. Slocum backed away and found a path leading up to the canyon rim above him. Occasionally glancing over his shoulder to be sure he hadn't been spotted by the guard smoking like a steam engine, Slocum reached the rim and got a view of the entire valley beyond the lake.

He sucked in his breath. The Circle C land was lush, with cattle grazing peacefully. About a half mile off stood a house smaller than Slocum would have thought a man of Campbell's temperament would have built. Beyond lay a barn and a corral with several dozen horses in it.

Slocum wedged himself between two rocks, took out a sheet of paper and began making a map of the Circle C spread. He sketched in the house, the pastureland and especially the lake. The inside of the dam had been coated with dirt, telling Slocum the river had originally been diverted down the underground tunnel while work proceeded on the dam. Then Campbell had plugged the tunnel and diverted all the water into a lake behind the dam.

The burning Wyoming sun and the dearth of rain had evaporated the lake below the overflow tunnel.

Slocum finished his map and tucked it inside his shirt. As he stood, he heard the crunch of boots on gravel. He froze. The sounds came from his right, from along the path following the canyon rim. His hand slowly moved to the ebony handle of his six-gun, but he didn't draw.

Two guards walked toward him.

Slocum sank down slowly, only partially hidden from the trail. He saw the tops of the men's hats and knew he would be discovered.

They stopped, giving Slocum the chance to creep back down into the crevice a tad more, but he was exposed. If the sentries looked his way, he would be discovered.

"Can't believe Marsh disappears like that," said one guard. "Makes his old man crazy."

"Mr. Campbell doesn't need Marsh to make him crazy. I swear, since he had us build this dam, he's been out of his mind."

"Water on the brain," said the first man, laughing. "But we got water and they don't."

"I had kin down there in town," said the second. "They moved on over to Cheyenne so I won't likely see 'em again for a long, long time."

"You're doin' all right here, Jed. Don't go thinkin' up reasons to cut and run. You know what Mr. Campbell thinks of quitters. Besides, we got good jobs. He pays us, feeds us and where else in this whole damn territory are you likely to get your fill of water?"

Slocum saw the men walk slowly past. Neither turned toward him. He remained as frozen as a fawn facing a mountain lion. Any gunplay now would bring all of Campbell's men down on his neck.

He half pulled his six-gun from its holster when one man turned in his direction. Luck was with Slocum. The man's partner moved at the same time, cutting off a direct line of sight.

"I wish things was like they were before it stopped rainin'," said the man with his back to Slocum.

"There's always gonna be trouble in town," said the one almost facing him.

"Yeah, we're gonna have to pry the deeds out of Harlow's dead hand some day soon. There's no way the two of them will ever make peace."

"Who's the biggest dog in the fight?" said the other, sighing. "Come on, let's chow down. I'm so hungry my belly's howlin' like a lovesick coyote."

His partner made an obscene observation, and the two continued along the path. Slocum reckoned the narrow trail wound down the side on the mountain and came out somewhere west of the lake's shoreline. From there it would be an easy hike over to the main house. The bunkhouse and maybe mess for the hands had to lie farther west, hidden by the numerous green, leafy cottonwoods that sprang up everywhere.

Slocum relaxed and let his six-shooter slip back into the holster. He pried himself out of the tight crevice and made sure the two guards had rounded a bend and were out of sight. How long he should wait worried him. He was anxious to return to Dehydration but not anxious to enter the tight, dark overflow tunnel or be seen by the men. If two of them were ready to grab some grub, others might, too.

Flopping belly down, Slocum studied the rock shelf that stretched just above the hole leading to the far side of the dam. Distant voices made him look to the far side of the lake. The two men sauntered along, jostling one another as they went to get their evening meal. Slocum let them vanish from sight, spending the time to study the inner wall of the dam. Every detail of its construction got filed away in his head. It would all come in handy if his plan worked.

Checking again to be sure the two guards were out of sight, Slocum slid down the face of the rock, got his toes on the shelf and slowly lowered himself.

Then he found himself flying through the air. His toes had slipped on unexpectedly wet rock. He plunged downward into the lake, landing with a splash that could be heard all the way back to Dehydration.

16

Slocum hit the water and sank straight down. He let a stream of bubbles escape his lips and instantly felt his lungs begin to burn. With a strong kick he pushed himself toward the rock wall and then slithered upward to the surface. He broke through, sputtering and gasping for breath. Try as he might, though, there was no place for him to grab onto. Thick green slime prevented him from holding on to support himself.

He slid back underwater. This time there wasn't a ten-foot plunge to take his breath away. He scissored his way back to the surface, taking time to look around to see if his unintentional swim had been noticed.

It had.

Slocum yanked off his hat and shoved it underwater, then sank so that only his face remained above water. Two curious guards atop the dam ambled along, looking down.

"You think we're gettin' catfish in there?" asked one.

His partner answered, "I hope so. I'm getting sick of eating beef. Whenever a cow dies, we get it for the next month on our plates. A piece of catfish would be a mighty fine change."

"With cornbread," said the first guard. "And maybe some collard greens."

Slocum hovered just underwater until the pair of them left, discussing culinary likes and dislikes. He broke the surface again, panting for breath. It had been so long since his clothes had been washed he had forgotten how heavy water-soaked duds could be. Worse, he wasn't used to taking a plunge with his boots and gun belt on.

Swimming slowly to keep from making a splash, Slocum dog-paddled to a sandy spit and flopped onto it. He sat for a few minutes, worrying constantly that he would be seen. Eventually he got his strength back. While he dried off, he scouted the rock face leading to the drainage hole and safety. With a little luck he could scale the wall up to the rock ledge above it again and then swing down as he had tried before.

Slocum felt the crush of time. He had been lucky so far with two pairs of sentries missing him. He doubted his luck would hold a third time. Moving carefully, he regained the ledge and sat on it, feet dangling over the edge. Visualizing where he had to go, Slocum kicked out, twisted in midair and thrust his feet forward. They hit dead center of the hole, and he found himself sliding along the water-worn floor all the way down a slope where he landed in a pile.

Behind, he heard voices again.

"Gotta be about the biggest catfish ever, I tell ya!"

The voices died down again as Slocum lay in a heap, waiting, waiting, waiting for the guards to find the hole and shoot into it. The bullets never came. Slocum wrung out his clothes the best he could, then retrieved his burlap bag and put a new candle into the miner's lamp. It took him several minutes to strike a lucifer and get the wick burning because the tin with his matches had been soaked, too, but luckily it had remained watertight.

He began the long trip back to where he had left his horse, every foot of the way a mile.

"Might be the only way the town's going to survive," Slocum said. He watched Pete Tahlmann closely for any sign the man was going to disagree. While the storekeeper wasn't enthusiastic, he wasn't about to deny Slocum was right. He couldn't. It was both obvious and the truth.

"Getting Harlow to meet with Trent Campbell is a stretch," Tahlmann said, rubbing his gray-stubbled chin. "It'd take a real diplomat to convince both of 'em to get together."

"But they both get what they want this way," Slocum said. "Harlow gets water back into town, which will draw in settlers to buy the land he's already bought up cheap and Campbell gets the town renamed for him. All Campbell has to do is sell the water to Harlow."

"That sneaky bastard Harlow'll sell it to the rest of us at a premium," Tahlmann said.

"Better than what you've got now—a dying town."

"Can't say that's not so, but this seems mighty dubious to me. Campbell only needs to wait till everyone's gone, then make Harlow an offer for dry land. Harlow's such a greedy bastard he'll go along."

"If the drought lasts that long," Slocum pointed out. "Harlow might hold on for a year or two but if the drought lasts longer, he has a lot of money tied up in worthless land. Settlers and ranchers will have moved on to where they can get their water."

"Drought could last that long," Tahlmann said agreeably. Then he shook his head. "Gettin' the pair of them together's like throwing kerosene into a fire. You might get heat but more likely you get an explosion that'll burn off your whiskers and singe your eyebrows."

"You might sweeten the deal with that five-thousand-dollar reward," Slocum suggested.

This startled Tahlmann.

"What's got into you, boy? Why are you giving up on the reward for bringin' water back to Dehydration?"

Slocum put on his best poker face.

"I only want to do what's right for the town."

"Bullshit. You're playin' some other game. What is it?"

"What could it be?" Slocum asked. "I'm not making a claim on the money. All I'm doing is suggesting a way you might solve your problems."

"Don't know either of those cantankerous sons of bitches would go along with meeting face-to-face, much less coming to an agreement. But what's there to lose?"

"That's the spirit," Slocum said. "How are you going to approach them?"

Tahlmann turned somber and sucked at his gums before finally answering.

"Don't much like it, but if I ask Annabelle, she'll get them together for a meal. That might be the only way."

"Annabelle?"

"Mrs. Jenkins. Both them varmints are sweet on her, but she won't have anything to do with them."

"Because she's already staked out her claim on somebody else," Slocum said, grinning.

"Might be, might not be," Tahlmann said. "Let me ask her. Might be tomorrow 'fore I get an answer out of her."

"No hurry," Slocum said. "The drought's not going to break anytime soon. Certainly not by tomorrow morning." Slocum figured he could use a rest before the real fun began.

"Those two surely can pack away the grub," Tahlmann said, sitting in the chair next to Slocum on the boardinghouse porch. "But then Annabelle's peach cobbler's mighty good."

"Dried peaches?"

"This year," Tahlmann admitted. "A Navajo peddler came through with a wagonload of dried peaches a few months back. That don't matter. She knows how to make it hot and tasty."

Slocum leaned back and pressed his ear against the wall of the boardinghouse. Having Annabelle Jenkins lure Harlow and Campbell to the dinner table might not have been such a good idea, Slocum thought now. He wanted to stir up matters in Dehydration, but bringing it all down to a shooting war hadn't been his intent. From the way Trent Campbell shouted at Eustace Harlow, the cemetery might have a new resident soon.

Still, it was worth the stirring to see if the pot boiled. Mostly, it was the only way Slocum could see to get Campbell into town so he could speak to him.

"You're a thief, Harlow!" shouted Campbell. The men came onto the porch and stood nose to nose like two fighters ready to begin a bare knuckles match.

"If I'm a thief, what's that make you? I didn't build that dam and choke off the water this town needs to survive."

"You changed the name."

"After you cut off the water. Why should we call this place Campbell when it was Trent Campbell who killed it?"

"Dehydration is no fit name for a town. Any town, even one as damned annoying as this one."

"It's annoying because it was named after you."

"Gents, set yourselves down and let's have a postprandial smoke," Tahlmann said amiably. "I got a box of ceegars from the store. Might be a tad on the dry side from bein' on my shelf so long, but there wasn't time to soak them in any fine brandy to moisten 'em up."

"I can use a smoke." Campbell dropped down so hard in a chair it creaked and threatened to collapse under him. Harlow stalked around and took a chair on the far side of Slocum so he could glare at all three of the other men—but mostly at Campbell.

"Wouldn't do any good soaking them in fine brandy," grumbled Harlow. "There's none to be had in all of Wyoming."

"It's up on the Circle C. I got a case in from France."

Slocum saw the bickering wasn't going to end.

"It sounds to me as if you're not coming to an agreement about the water," he said. "You're not going to sell it and even if you did, Harlow wouldn't meet your price. Does that about sum it up, Mr. Campbell?"

"Shoulda shot you when I had the chance," Campbell said. "You and the rest of that ragtag posse of yours."

"Keep talkin' like that, Trent, and you can forget the ceegar," Tahlmann said.

"Stuff your cigar. I'm going home. Thank Annabelle for the fine dinner. I wish she'd come to her senses and cook for me up at the Circle C. She'd have plenty of water there." Campbell turned his back on them, then spat and walked to the far end of the porch.

"You—" Harlow sputtered incoherently, got to his feet and stormed off into the night.

"So much for a meeting of the minds," Tahlmann said.

Slocum hurried behind Campbell, blocking his retreat unless he vaulted the railing into the yard.

"It would have worked for everyone concerned. You don't need all the water, and it would have kept the town alive."

"No telling how long this drought's going to last. One back in the '60s lasted damned near eight years. I need the water for the Circle C, for my cattle."

"Mrs. Jenkins could use some of that water just sitting behind the dam."

"She can have all she wants. All she needs to do is ask me, though I'm not too inclined toward her at the moment. Not after she tricked me into having dinner with that sharper!"

"What about Maddy Villareal?" Slocum asked.

"Her? What's she got to do with this? Bah! What's the difference? You tell that gold digger to stay away from my son. She should never have come back."

Slocum stared at Trent Campbell's back as the man stalked off, his body set the same way that Harlow's had been. They were peas in a pod. But that did the town no good.

And it didn't answer any of Slocum's questions about Marsh and Maddy.

17

Slocum waited for Annabelle Jenkins to leave immediately after dinner. From the way she moved about, carrying a small grip, he figured she was going to spend the night with one of her many suitors. After she rattled off in her buggy, Slocum went to the front door and started to knock. His knuckles stopped a mere inch from the wood.

Maddy was alone inside. He wanted to clear the air with her and find out what Trent Campbell had really meant. Somehow, she figured into his anger and desire to dam up the river so Dehydration turned into a ghost town and blew away on a high wind.

Opening the front door, he slipped inside. He heard Maddy singing out back. He glanced up the stairs in the direction of her bedroom, then hurried through the house in the direction of the songbird sounds. Slocum stopped and stared when he saw the kitchen door standing open. Maddy had heated water on the stove and had carried it out to a galvanized tub on the back porch, where she luxuriated in the hot bath. Long black hair dangled down as she leaned back, resting her head on the edge. Her eyes were closed and her hands moved slowly in the soapy water, causing tiny waves to ripple from side to side and break over her bare breasts, which poked up delightfully. Slocum stood and watched for a few seconds, then quietly unfastened his gun belt and kicked off his boots.

Maddy stirred at the faint sounds he made.

"Who's there?" She half sat up in the bath and looked around. The suds dripped sedately down her body, highlighting her luscious curves. Not seeing anyone, she flopped back into the tub with a sigh and began singing again.

Slocum shucked his shirt, dropped his hat and pants and moved to a spot behind her. Maddy's long damp hair trailed down outside the tub. Slocum began stroking it. Maddy stirred and stopped singing, then sat up again.

"Who—John!"

"Good to see you," he said, gazing at her naked beauty. Her eyes were fixed at his groin and the fleshy flagpole jutting up there.

"It's good to see you up and about, too," she said. "How long have you been spying on me?"

"Long enough," he said.

"Oh, yes it is, but I asked how long you'd been playing Peeping Tom?"

He moved around the tub and perched on one sharp edge. She reached out and curled her fingers around him, squeezing gently and then moving up and down slowly.

"So you don't go anywhere," she explained, a wicked grin dancing on her ruby lips.

"You worry I'd be fool enough to want to go anywhere else?"

"I'd invite you into the tub but there's not enough room."

He reached into the warm, soapy water and stroked along the inside of her thigh. She sighed and tensed her hand around him to show she enjoyed his light, teasing caress.

"You're right," he said. "The tub seems all full up. But I like what's filling it up."

"And I'd this filling me," she said, tugging on his manhood. Maddy bent forward and kissed the very tip. Then her tongue flicked out and stroked the underside all the way down. A chill passed through Slocum, in spite of the warm night. He carefully stood so he wouldn't dislodge her, stepped across and straddled the tub. He settled back down, his feet flat on the floor on either side, his groin even with the lovely woman's mouth.

She gobbled and sucked and licked and kissed until Slocum was about ready to explode like some young buck out for the first time. The woman's educated mouth knew all the right spots—and Maddy wasn't shy about using her tongue, lips and teeth.

"This is fine, but I want to do more for you," Slocum said, fighting to keep his voice from cracking with strain. She did not stop mouthing him as he talked. He guessed that she took secret delight in trying to make him gasp and moan for more. Slocum was at the point of giving her the pleasure of hearing those incoherent sounds when she rocked back in the tub. The water sloshed out onto the porch floor, running down his legs to get there.

"I want more, too," she said in a dreamy, husky voice.

Slocum backed away reluctantly and knelt at the foot of the tub. He reached under the water, caught slender ankles and pulled. He got both her legs up out of the tub and over his shoulders. Then he bent down and kissed at those tasty melons that had beguiled him when he had blundered onto her bathing so provocatively.

Maddy kept her arms on the sides of the tub and lifted her rump off the bottom so he could work down a ways on her body, to her belly, to her navel, lower. Slocum's tongue lashed out, but all he tasted was soap. He hardly noticed because of his erotic pursuit. But the position was too uncomfortable for both of them. He could not reach the places he wanted—and that she did, also.

He slid his hands around under her lathered buttocks

and hoisted her out of the tub. This slid her hips forward and, with her legs still over his shoulders, her privates came within tongue range. Slocum lapped and licked and thrust with his tongue until Maddy's legs tightened down on either side of his head, turning him delightfully deaf and blind. His entire world was at the end of his nose—and the tip of his tongue. She began trembling and leaned forward, but this took her away from his lips.

Slocum stood slowly, lifting her bodily. As he reached up to support her, the woman's well-soaped sleek skin betrayed him. Her legs widened and she slid down around him until they were pressed chest to chest. Slocum kissed her hard, and she returned it. His hands roved her slippery, sensuous body and found sensitive spots he hardly imagined that sent tremors all through her.

"John, oh, John, I can't stand any more," she said. "I need you now."

He reared back, then shifted weight so she moved from him. He quickly spun her around and let her drop to her knees outside the tub. As she bent forward, her nipples brushed lightly over the warm, lapping waves in the galvanized tub.

"Oh, that feels so good."

He said nothing as he dropped to his knees behind her and moved forward. His hands stroked over the sleek curves of her rump, then slid around her body to hold her into position. He wiggled a bit, thrust forward and found the gates leading to paradise. The very tip of his hardness knocked on those nether doors, then slowly entered when she began rolling her hips about.

Inch by delightfully slow inch he entered her from behind. Maddy bent forward, her breasts sinking out of sight in the bath water. She gripped the edges of the tub and began rotating her hips in a deliberate circle, first one way, then the other. This stirred Slocum's rod, now buried fully within her tightness.

Slocum clung to her wet body, reached around and stroked over her belly and then moved provocatively lower. As he touched a particularly sensitive nub of flesh, Maddy gasped. Her hips went wild, thrashing about. Slocum hung on like he was riding a bucking bronco. Sweat ran down Slocum's body from the effort of maintaining his position deep within her core, not moving, letting her proceed as she saw fit. But the pulse in his temples hammered away now, and every thud of his heart sent an earthquake down his length.

"I can feel you, John. I can feel your heart beating all through my insides," she said in a weak voice. "It excites me so."

He stoked over her thighs, her belly, between her legs, all the while remaining buried deeply. But when he bent over to kiss her back and outline each and every bone in her spine with his tongue, he felt her powerful inner muscles clamp down. She shuddered again. And this time there was no holding back. A white-hot tide built within his loins that would not be denied.

Slocum began stroking, moving in and out so that carnal heat built along the entire length of his fleshy shaft. He tried to keep the movement rhythmic but failed quickly. She wore at his control until he wanted only to sink into sweet oblivion. He moved faster, with more irregular strokes, and finally he let out an animal howl when she slammed herself backward as he drove forward.

His seed spilled, and then he sank down to his heels. Maddy still hung over the edge of the tub, her deliciously rounded moons facing him. He kissed them each in turn. Then the woman swung up and around.

"You look all sweaty," she said, out of breath. Her naked breasts rose and fell as her chest heaved to draw in enough air. "I'll be happy to wash you off."

"Why not?" Slocum said. "You already got me off."

Maddy laughed and stepped into the tub, kneeling. He

faced her and crouched down the best he could. This was uncomfortable, but he wasn't complaining, not with her slender fingers sloshing water all over him. When she found the bar of soap and began lathering his hide, Slocum felt himself relaxing all over.

He returned the favor, relishing the flow of her bare flesh under his hands. Then she silently stepped from the tub and picked up a towel. Mopping the water off one another was as much fun as the bathing.

"Your clothes are filthy," she said with some disdain when they had completely dried each other. "But there's nothing to do about that."

"Not that dirty," Slocum said, remembering the dunking he had taken earlier in the lake behind Trent Campbell's dam.

"Dirty enough." She began dressing but she did so slowly, putting on a show for him as she bent, turned and slithered into her clothing. Slocum was quicker getting into his clothes. There was no way he could match her sexy performance.

"What brings you around?" she asked once she had completely dressed.

"You."

"You certainly brought me around," Maddy said. "I meant, why'd you come over tonight?"

Slocum saw no reason to pussyfoot about so he came right out and asked, "What's Marsh Campbell to you?"

"Why, he's a terrible man."

"Because his father forbade him from seeing you, and he obeyed his father?"

Slocum knew he had hit the bull's-eye from the way Maddy flushed.

"You used to live here, back when the town was named Campbell. You and Marsh hit it off. Might be you wanted him to marry you."

"He wanted to marry me," the fiery woman said, "but

his father said I was a nothing, a half-breed because my father was Mexican and my mother was Irish. They were rich and owned a rancho in New Mexico. They were also killed by the Navajos, our hacienda burned and all our livestock stolen. I barely escaped with my life, much less any of the family fortune."

"Trent Campbell thought you were after his son only for the position it would give you when it came to owning the Circle C?"

"Yes." The way she spoke was more like a snake hissing than a gorgeous woman speaking.

"So when Marsh wouldn't marry you, you left town? Or did they drive you out?"

"I left in embarrassment," she said. Maddy thrust out her chin and showed the defiance that drew Slocum to her. This was not a woman who ever gave up on what she wanted. "I left but I swore on my parents' souls to return with money of my own so even the rich Trent Campbell could not claim I wanted his son for their money!"

"The reward for the dowsing," Slocum said. "That's what you want the five thousand dollars for, to lord it over Trent Campbell. What then?"

Maddy didn't answer, but Slocum read the expression that fluttered across her face. She still loved Marsh, and it was probably mutual.

"Marsh is a fool if he chose a ranch over you," Slocum said.

"Don't talk of him that way! You don't know!"

This outburst confirmed what Slocum suspected. She would marry Marsh in a heartbeat. He didn't know the young rancher that well, in spite of having saved his life, but Slocum thought he was spineless, not standing up to his father's demands.

Slocum would have spit in Trent Campbell's eye, but then he wasn't the old rancher's son and was going to do it in a roundabout way, anyhow.

"You ought to try dowsing for water again, up near where we got out of that tunnel," Slocum said.

"But it is dry. We walked in it for miles. There wasn't enough water in the bottom to make decent mud."

"If you have the witchy skill to dowse, you've got to look out there again. No telling what you might find."

"All right," Maddy said. "I intended to try other places, but if you insist, I'll go back to that area. Will you come with me?"

"Get Pete Tahlmann or Benjamin at the saloon. They'd jump at the chance to roam around the prairie with you."

"Where're you going?"

Slocum only smiled, then kissed her before he left. He had miles to ride and deals to make before dawn.

18

"With their dying breath, they'll string you up," Slocum said, looking intently at Conrad Ballantine to see how the man accepted such a flat-out lie.

"I'm trying to help!"

"I know that, you know that, but those folks are at the end of their rope."

"You mean my rope." Ballantine ran his fingers over his throat, about where a length of hemp would tighten into a noose.

"They've done about everything, and they're not going to put up with another attempt. In fact, you set off even one stick of the dynamite and they might come after you."

"Even if I got it to rain?"

"They won't believe a few sticks of dynamite did the trick when you floated that balloon with an entire crate and it didn't work."

"Five thousand dollars is a powerful lot to turn my back on," Ballantine said, scratching his head. "To just wheel my wagon around and leave means I've failed—my theories have failed. I'm so sure this will work, given a fair chance."

"They'll hang you in the rain and not think twice on it,"

Slocum assured him. "I'll help you out, though. How much dynamite do you have left?"

"Only a crate—call it twenty sticks."

"Fuse and blasting caps, too?"

Ballantine nodded.

"Sell it all to me, and I'll get rid of it for you. I can't pay much, but ten dollars ought to get you well on the road to Cheyenne or Big Piney."

"Big Piney's down south. Heard-tell it rains there on occasion. Might be a better place to try my experiment. But then I wouldn't have any dynamite."

Slocum knew then that Ballantine was dickering. The ebb and flow of their dealing ended with Slocum giving the crackpot experimenter twenty dollars in greenbacks.

"Thank you kindly, Slocum," the experimenter said. "You want help deliverin' the dynamite?"

"Help?"

"You've got some specific place in mind for it, don't you?"

Slocum had to laugh.

"You can drive me a few miles that way," Slocum said, jerking his thumb over his shoulder in the direction of the mountains. This saved him the trouble of loading the crate onto his Appaloosa and getting it to the hole where he had ventured to Campbell's dam and the lake behind it.

It took the better part of an hour for Ballantine to reach the spot. Slocum was glad to see the two ropes he had left dangling in the hole were still in place. He used one to lower the crate of explosives into the dry underground waterway.

"Hope our paths cross again, Slocum," Ballantine said, looking around. "I think it'd be mighty good for me to start driving and not stop until I hear a big bang." Ballantine started to ask what Slocum was up to, then shook his head, got into his wagon and waved as he drove off.

Slocum knew he had a considerable chore ahead of him. He lowered himself into the hole, considered leaving his Colt Navy, gun belt and Stetson behind because he knew the way the subterranean channel narrowed in places, then decided that he might need the firepower at the other end. And his Stetson, battered though it was, had cost him eight dollars in Omaha. He wasn't going to leave a perfectly good hat behind. In addition, it protected his head when he got careless with the low ceilings in the tunnel.

He used his knife to fashion a yoke out of part of the rope, stashed what he could in the burlap bag, readied his miner's candle in the lantern, lit it and then took a deep breath. It was a long way to duck, walk and crawl to get to the Circle C lake.

Slocum pulled himself up the slope to the mouth of the tunnel and peered out. It had taken most of the night to drag the crate of dynamite all the way from the cave-in to this spot. The predawn dankness made his task both a little easier and a little harder.

He wasn't as likely to be seen by the vigilant sentries as he placed his charges, but finding the proper spots for the dynamite would be chancy in the dark. Dropping onto his belly, he looked down into the lake. He saw a few holes just at the waterline, which might be of help, but he needed more than a big explosion with a lot of dust and rock being kicked into the air. He had worked in mines long enough to learn a bit about being a powder monkey, but wished he had more time and the freedom to chisel a few deep holes into the rock.

The water had smoothed the rock and dug the tunnel he had traversed, but it had done this over long centuries. He wanted to change it all in a heartbeat with a single big bang. Slocum slid back down the slope inside the tunnel and examined the floor. It was slick but had pockets where the water had dissolved or eroded softer rock. He pried and poked and found several pockets a yard down the slope that might take a stick of dynamite each.

He planted the sticks but did not place either caps or fuse on them. The real chore was going to be blowing out the lip of the tunnel all the way down to the surface of the lake—and farther. He wanted the newly blasted tunnel to open several feet below the surface of the present lake. Even more would be best.

In the process he didn't want to disturb Trent Campbell's dam too much. If the dam broke, the Sulphur River would return to its original bed but all that would happen then would be the rancher rebuilding the dam and making the residents of Dehydration even madder. Nobody gained from a sporadic flow that could be cut off again.

Slocum left his gun, boots and hat behind as he dropped from the tunnel mouth into the lake. He slid underwater as silently as a shadow crossing a room and worked more by sense of touch than sight as he worked down the rock face beneath the tunnel.

More than an hour passed as he repeatedly dove, hunting for the proper spots to plant the remainder of his dynamite. Resting occasionally, he crimped the blasting cap and added lengths of the black miner's fuse. It had surprised Slocum the first time he had seen the fuse burn underwater; it had saved his and a blasting engineer's life in the Comstock. Hot water had poured into the mine where they were working and their escape had been blocked. The engineer said all he needed was for the lucifer that lit the fuse to be dry. The rest of the explosion, dynamite, fuse and cap, could be underwater. And they had been. The resulting explosion in such tight quarters had deafened Slocum for a week, but they had escaped the mine and the boiling water coming up from the very bowels of hell.

Swimming in Campbell's lake was far more salubrious. The cool water eased the aches and scrapes he had acquired during his long crawl to this spot. After Slocum had made a dozen or more dives and tamped in the dynamite below the lake's waterline, he surfaced, gathered the long fuses and pulled them back down the tunnel to a safe spot where he could light the bundle.

As he pulled out his tin of lucifers from the burlap bag, he stopped.

"Damnation," he muttered. He had concentrated so hard on planting the sticks of dynamite he had overlooked one vital fact.

If he lit the fuses and the ploy worked, water would rush through the very tunnel he now sat in. There was no way he could ever outrun the water. The only way he would survive drowning was if his plan failed.

Slocum cursed his own single-minded approach to the problem, then quieted and thought about what to do. Even if he added a considerable length to the fuses, he could never wiggle back through the tunnel in time to avoid the rush of water from the lake filling the subterranean channel again. That meant he couldn't be anywhere near the blast when it went off and certainly not in the tunnel.

He packed his gear, then repositioned the long length of fuse leading to the bundle of other fuses. Burning at exactly one foot per minute, he estimated he had more than five minutes before the bundle of fusing caught. From there he had another five to eight minutes before the dynamite began detonating.

"Ten minutes," he muttered, laying the fuse up on the ledge above the tunnel. "Thirteen minutes and no more."

He fixed the end of the fuse to the ledge with a large rock, then skinned up and out of the tunnel and pulled himself to the ledge. Sitting with his back against the cold stone face of the cliff, he waited to see if the noise he'd made drew unwanted attention. Wherever the guards patrolled, it wasn't along this section of the canyon rim or along the ragged top of Campbell's dam.

Slocum took a deep breath, struck a lucifer and applied it to the end of the fuse. It sizzled and popped, then began burning down to the blasting caps. He left the burlap bag behind, stood and climbed to the trail along the canyon wall. Slocum scouted the area quickly, then started across the dam to the far side. He had no idea if there was a trail down the canyon face on this side but knew there had to be one on the other. Marsh Campbell had ridden up along it days before.

Halfway across the dam, Slocum froze. He heard two sounds. The fuse hissing as it burned—and the crunch of boots on loose rock. He turned slowly and saw that a guard had worked his way down to the ledge. From here, the sentry could see the dynamite and easily pluck the fuses from the bundles of explosive.

Slocum reversed his course and raced back to the point where he could follow the guard.

Before Slocum could slide down, the guard called up, "Sound the alarm! It's happenin' like the boss said. They're tryin' to blow the dam!"

"I'll help," Slocum said, muffling his voice the best he could.

"Who's there? That you, Clay?"

"Yeah."

"You're not Clay!" the guard cried. "Help! Intruder! We got dynamite behind the dam!"

Slocum lost his balance on the gravel and fell to his butt, slipping back toward the ledge feet-first. Not even trying, he sent both his boots into the guard's face. Trying to balance on the narrow stone ledge and failing, the guard toppled backward. Slocum saw the man's arms flapping like he was some kind of giant bird struggling to take flight. Then he splashed loudly into the lake.

Along with the guard went the end of the fuse.

Slocum made a grab for it and missed. Then he knew it didn't matter. The fuse had been designed to burn underwater. And it did. He could see the dim speck of burning coal creeping along the waxy black fuse toward the hidden dynamite underwater.

The guard was splashing around, crying for help and attracting attention. He had forgotten about the fuse in his attempt to get to solid ground. Slocum wondered if the man could swim. He wasn't about to go help him if he couldn't, not with the dynamite so close to detonating.

Scrambling back up the cliff face to the trail, Slocum retraced his steps to the middle of the dam. Before he reached the far side and the trail's dubious end down on the canyon floor below the dam, he saw two more dark silhouettes coming toward him.

"Down there!" Slocum shouted, pointing to the guard churning around in the lake. "Clay's fallen in."

"I'm Clay," came the cold voice from one of the men blocking his path.

Slocum saw the guards going for their six-shooters. He could draw and fire, but in the dark he had to hit both of them. All they had to do was for one of them to wing him and he'd be dead. Putting his head down and making himself as small a target as possible, Slocum ran forward like a charging bull. He slammed into the two men, shoulders catching them both in the belly and bowling them over. Stumbling, Slocum fell to his knees. He didn't try to stand. Instead, he swung around, picked up a rock the size of his fist and slammed it down into the middle of the shadowy figure on the ground.

The shock of the rock hitting bone resonated all the way up to his shoulder.

A bullet sang over his head. Slocum fell forward over the downed, unconscious guard and lay still.

"Damnation, did I kill you, Clay?" cried the second guard. "I was aiming at him. I didn't mean—"

The guard incautiously approached, fearful of having shot his partner by accident. When he came close enough, Slocum threw dirt and small gravel he had scooped up into the air and into the man's face. The man fired a second time in reaction. He never got a chance to fire a third time.

Slocum wrapped his arms around the man's knees and heaved, picking him up and tossing him in the direction of the still-screaming guard in the lake.

Slocum saw the guard he had attacked flying through the air and the splash as he hit the lake a dozen yards from the first guard. Slocum tried to catch sight of the bright spark burning along the fuse, but he was too far away. He had to trust that the big bundle of fuses would ignite and set off all the dynamite simultaneously.

Scrambling to keep his balance, he started down the dark path winding along the canyon rim. He fell several times and wished he had a miner's candle to light the way. But that would have been a giveaway—a dead giveaway. He would have been an easy target from ahead or anywhere along the far rim. Worse than being a target, though, was the chance he might miss the trail down the side of the canyon wall. He couldn't see the darkness-shrouded canyon floor for any landmarks. And he had never followed the trail down from above. His single abortive attempt going up the trail had been met with intense rifle fire.

Behind he heard an alarm bell ringing. The two guards dunked in the lake had finally attracted the attention of those up in the Circle C bunkhouse.

Slocum kept moving, setting as good a pace as he could.

In his rush Slocum missed a dark spot that moved just enough to betray itself as another guard.

Slocum passed the point, then froze when a cold voice called out, "I got a rifle aimed at yer back. Take another step and I'll fill you full of lead."

Slocum stopped and raised his hands.

"Turn around. I don't want to shoot nobody in the back."

"So you're going to shoot me in cold blood?"

"Thought entered my mind. Don't know if the boss won't give me a bigger reward if you're dead instead of alive."

Slocum turned slowly, judging his chances of drawing and firing. He couldn't see the guard clearly but knew there was a rifle already aimed at him. Even if they were both shooting in the dark, the sentry had a better chance of ventilating Slocum than the other way around.

Then the world moved. The ground heaved and a shower of water cascaded down on both Slocum and the guard. Slocum had been expecting the dynamite to go off eventually. The guard had no warning at all.

The shock wave and the sudden rain gave Slocum the chance to rush forward in attack, but he didn't have to. The guard had jerked around in surprise and fell down the side of the canyon.

But he didn't fall far. Slocum saw him writhing about in pain a dozen feet below. The guard had been posted at the top of the trail leading from the canyon floor. Slocum would have missed it entirely if the guard hadn't stopped him.

Jumping down, Slocum hit the trail and got to the side of the guard. The man was sitting up, moaning and shaking his head. Slocum measured the distance and kicked hard. The toe of his boot connected with the man's chin, snapping his head back and putting him out like a light. Slocum grabbed the fallen rifle and slipped and slid down the steep trail, intent on reaching the canyon floor as quickly as possible. The alarm bell back at the Circle C ranch continued to ring. Every cowboy in Campbell's employ had to be awake, armed and ready to fight now.

Slocum wished he could see if his scheme had worked. Since there wasn't a torrent of water roaring down the canyon, filling the dry riverbed, that much of his plan had worked. The dam was still intact. But had he blown away enough rock around the tunnel mouth to let water from the lake flood the subterranean channel again?

He couldn't tell, and going back would be pure suicide. Trent Campbell had to be chewing nails and spitting tacks by now. If he caught the man responsible for this attack on his private citadel and stolen lake, hanging might not be the end of it.

More than once Slocum almost pitched over the verge to his death. The trail proved more narrow than he had suspected, seeing Marsh Campbell go up it. But he came to a widening—almost five yards between rock wall and the edge of the trail—and he stopped. The gunmen who had fired on him when he had followed Marsh had been stationed somewhere on the trail. This would be a perfect spot.

"The boss wants everyone up on top. Now!" Slocum called. He waited for a moment to see if there might still be guards lying in wait here.

Seeing nothing move, he walked out into the middle of the wide, open space and knew he had made a big mistake.

The click of at least three six-guns cocking greeted him.

"We seen you comin' down the trail and knowed it wasn't none of us," said a hidden guard. "What all's been goin' on up there?"

"Don't expect an answer out of him. Not the truth, at least," growled another guard. "He's causin' all the ruckus."

"Let's take him on up so's the boss can deal with him."

Slocum had no idea where either of the men were hidden. Then came something entirely unexpected.

"What's wrong with you, boys? Don't you recognize him? He's the new hand we hired a couple days back."

"Didn't know we hired nobody."

"Put your guns down." A section of rock split open, and a man walked out to greet Slocum, hand extended. "Good of you to come with the message, Sam."

Slocum shook Marsh Campbell's hand.

"Get on up and help out, like Sam here asked. He and I'll watch the trail."

"Are you sure, Marsh?"

"Do it." Marsh Campbell's voice carried the same edge

as his father's. The two men jumped to obey, hurrying up the trail.

"Thanks," Slocum said in a low voice as Marsh pulled his hand back. "Why'd you speak up for me like that? You'll be in a whale of a lot of trouble when your pa hears about it."

"It's another half mile to the canyon. It'll take you a while in the dark, so you'd better get moving."

Slocum lit out. For some reason, he wasn't at all worried that Marsh Campbell would shoot him in the back, even though that would get the young man in good with his father.

It was after dawn when Slocum got back to Dehydration. He was dog-tired from his long crawl in the tunnel and the fight afterward, but he had too much to do before he could sleep. He got to doing it.

19

"What's the use?" Maddy Villareal said, heaving a deep sigh. Slocum reached out and grabbed her by the shoulders and forced her to look him squarely in the eye.

"You tried and failed. Try again. Don't you have any confidence in your skill? Was it all a sham, like Professor Leonardo's Water Extract?"

"That got the sulfur out of the water," she said. "I should never have come back. I'm leaving. There's nothing for me here."

"Run and you'll hate yourself forever," Slocum said. "You'll always wonder if things might have been different, and you'll never know the answer."

"I . . . I know they won't be different. How could they?"

"Between you and Marsh?"

"You leave him out of this," she flared.

"You love him, don't you?"

"No."

She said one thing, and Slocum heard another. He suspected that his easy escape from the Circle C, thanks to Marsh, had come for the same reason. Marsh loved her and wanted her to have what she desired most. Marsh thought that was Slocum. Slocum knew better.

"Once more. You remember the other night when I told you where? Try it along that area again."

"It's dry land. You said there weren't any green plants, and that that showed the underground river had gone dry all the way into the mountains."

Slocum held her by both arms until she tried to wiggle free. He tightened his grip, still saying nothing until he felt her sag a little in defeat.

"Oh, very well. I'll get my dowsing rod, but it won't help."

"How'd you learn to dowse?"

"There was a woman down in Taos who had great skill. She taught me, even gave me her best dowsing rod." Maddy's eyes drifted to the small case sitting on the table in the entryway of the boardinghouse. "She gave me the divining rod, and then she upped and died not a week later."

"You owe it to her memory to put your skills to use as much as you owe it to yourself to try again."

Maddy jerked free and opened the case, taking out the Y of birch wood. Her eyes widened a little when she gripped it.

"What's wrong?" Slocum asked.

"Nothing. It just felt strange. It jerked as I picked it up. It's never done that before."

"Go on, go dowse the town a new water supply," Slocum said. "The money'll be worthwhile, even if you don't stay in Dehydration."

"There wouldn't be any reason to call it that if I discovered water," she said. Then her jaw hardened, and Slocum knew what she was thinking. She would never stay if the city changed its name back to Campbell. She looked over her shoulder at Slocum. "Are you coming?"

"I'll be along shortly. You get started," he said.

"Very well." Maddy put on her big-brimmed sun hat and picked up the case where she had returned the birch divining rod. She left to get her buggy and drive out to the spot Slocum had steered her to. If everything had gone well, water from Campbell's lake flowed in the underground channel again. If the blast hadn't recreated the subterranean river, nothing was going to be lost.

But Slocum felt a curious optimism for the excursion that prodded him to get Tahlmann to join him when Maddy found the water. By the time he had rounded up the storekeeper and convinced him to accompany him out into the countryside, Slocum saw he had acquired a regular parade of people. They needed a holiday, and this break provided it. Slocum worried a mite that a town filled with people who thought hanging trials were a form of entertainment might get testy if Maddy didn't find the water, but he said nothing.

"What makes you so all-fired sure she's gonna find water today?" Tahlmann asked as they rode out in the man's buckboard. The prairie hadn't gotten any smoother or wetter, but Slocum felt a change in the air. And he remembered how Maddy's dowsing rod had responded when she had taken it from the case.

"Nothing much," Slocum said. "Just a hunch."

"Have anything to do with the explosion we heard last night?"

"Explosion?" Slocum asked, playing dumb.

"More 'n one, actually. Three or four just before sunup. Might have been blasting stumps up on the Circle C, but not even Trent Campbell's stupid enough to do it at night."

"No way of telling what's going on behind that dam," Slocum said.

"Thought maybe somebody had bought the rest of Conrad Ballantine's dynamite and blown up the dam, but I hustled on down to the Sulphur River and the bed was as dry as ever. Not so much as a drop extra comin' downriver."

"How's Harlow coming with his negotiations with Campbell to buy water for the town?"

"He quit. Harlow knows he can buy the land around

here cheap if there's no water, so he hasn't got much reason to pursue the matter. It was mighty sneaky of you gettin' them together, though. Might have worked if they hadn't always hated each other so much. Campbell has a way about him. His cattle are always the plumpest and fetch the highest prices, so he doesn't need Harlow's high percentage loans, but Campbell's not got enough money to buy out the bank, even if Harlow'd sell."

"The two of them would be the last men standing in a pissing contest," Slocum said.

"That's the Gospel truth," Tahlmann said. He spat, then sat a little straighter in the driver's box. "Maddy's already got quite a crowd out there."

They drove closer, then got down and pushed their way through the crowd to where Maddy stood with the birch Y in her hands, eyes closed.

"She won't find anything," Eustace Harlow said. "Can't. There's no water out here."

"That'd suit you jist fine, wouldn't it, banker man?" said Gus Ferguson. "You made offers to 'bout everyone to buy their land. If she finds water, the town'll thrive again."

"If that happens, I'll make even more money," Harlow said haughtily.

Slocum looked sharply at the banker. Something in Harlow's words didn't ring true.

"Less I miss my guess, there's not a hell of a lot of Dehydration he hasn't bought up already," Tahlmann said. "I'm holdin' out. So's Annabelle, but her and me might just take Harlow's money and go off together if we don't get water soon."

"Is she all right?" asked Jimmy.

"She looks like she got knocked in the head or somethin'," Eddie said, crowding close.

Maddy did look as if she was in terrible pain. Her face was contorted as she tried to pull away from the birch divining rod, but it seemed to have a life of its own, pulling her this way and that before finally leading her in the direction where Slocum suspected the underground channel ran. A bit before the spot he had scouted out, Maddy stopped. The tip of the dowsing rod pointed straight down.

"Here," she said in a choked voice. "Water's here. Lots and lots of water."

"Oh, don't be ridiculous," scoffed Harlow. "There's no water here."

Jimmy and Eddie had dropped to their knees and were scrabbling like prairie dogs digging a burrow. One of them held up a rock. It was damp. The other continued digging, throwing dirt behind him. Someone in the crowd stepped up and rubbed the dirt between his fingers.

"It's damp. There's water here!"

This set off a rush to the spot. Men clawed at the ground with their fingers as they sought life-giving water. Maddy stepped back, her face pale and drawn. Her ebon eyes opened and fixed on Slocum.

"Water," she mouthed. "Water!"

As her silent message went to Slocum a louder one was proclaimed when Eddie poked down far enough to produce a steady flow of water.

"We kin make our own lake here!" he cried, jumping to his feet and stomping in the mud. Others joined him, but Slocum saw how Harlow was backing off. The stricken look on the banker's face told the story. No matter what he'd said about wanting water to be found, Maddy's discovery terrified him.

"There's enough water for the whole town," Slocum told Tahlmann. "Does Maddy get the five-thousand-dollar reward?"

"Reckon so," Tahlmann said, seeing more water bubbling up from below. "Harlow's got it stashed in his bank for safekeeping."

"Harlow!" snapped Slocum. "Are you going to get Miss

Villareal her reward money? Or were you trying to hightail it out of town?"

"I, uh, yes, that's what I was doing. I was going to get the reward money. From the bank."

Slocum walked over to the banker, Tahlmann following close behind, to see what was going on.

"You don't have the money, do you?" Slocum asked. He read the truth in the banker's frightened expression. "What'd you do with the money?"

"I . . . I used it to buy up all the land around here. The businesses in town, the farms, even a goodly part of the Bar None ranch. They were selling for pennies! But now that there's water again, I can sell the property and give the money to Miss Villareal and—"

"No," Slocum said. "She wants her money *now*."

"I can't!" pleaded the banker. "I don't have it."

"You have deeds for all this land," Slocum said. "Sign those over to her."

"But she'd own three-quarters of Dehydration! And farmland and—"

"You remember that trial we put Slocum through after he killed your two henchmen in self-defense?" Tahlmann asked. "This time there wouldn't be a trial if he shot you. Fact is, I'd lead the parade for him. We might just have a week-long celebration, everyone takin' turns dancin' on your grave!"

"I can't give her that much land!"

"What's the phrase I heard 'em use down in New Mexico after a necktie party?" Slocum said. "Jerked to Jesus? That was it. Do you have enough money left, Harlow, for a decent funeral, if they'd put a hanged criminal in with decent folks in the town cemetery?"

"I . . . I'll do it, but it'll ruin me. I spent everything buying up the land. It's all mine."

"It's all Miss Villareal's, you mean," Tahlmann said.

"Slocum here'll convince her to take the land and property instead of cash, and nobody in these parts will know how a banker stole money that wasn't his from his own vault."

"And we'll forget who sent his two henchmen out to kidnap her when she came back to town," Slocum said. Harlow turned white as a bleached muslin sheet at this. Slocum knew he had guessed the identity of the men who had first accosted Maddy when she returned. The two were dead and buried, so they had paid. But Harlow needed to worry a bit more that Slocum would tell the townspeople that their lovely savior had almost been stolen away by their banker.

Slocum left Tahlmann and the banker to tell Maddy what had happened. He wasn't too surprised to see her and Marsh off a ways from the crowd that still slopped around in the mud like hogs in a wallow. But he also saw Trent Campbell making a beeline for Marsh and Maddy. Slocum cut him off.

"A fine day, isn't it, Campbell?"

"Why do you say that?"

"Miss Villareal found water. The town's going to prosper again because of it."

"You're the one! You blew the drain hole in the side of the canyon!"

"Might be someone helped nature take its true course again," Slocum said, "but the dam wasn't even cracked. You've still got your lake on Circle C land."

"And half the lake's gone, drained. And this is where the water ran!"

"Let it drop, Campbell," Slocum said. "And don't meddle in your son's affairs."

"He's too good to marry her kind," Campbell growled. "If he marries her, I'll disinherit him. He won't have a goddamned cent!"

"Won't matter much if Marsh marries her," Slocum said.

"What's that? Why not?"

"She's the new owner of most of Dehydration and land all the way onto the old Bar None spread."

"You're lying!" Campbell looked stunned.

"Even heard rumors of them renaming the town to Villareal. I think it's a right pretty name, don't you?" Slocum's cold green eyes bored into Campbell's. He backed the rancher down. Campbell snarled and swung into the saddle, riding off at a gallop toward his canyon and the ranch securely sequestered in it.

Tahlmann came up.

"You surely did put a burr under his saddle. What are you going to do now?" asked the storekeeper.

"Maybe go to a wedding." Slocum looked at Marsh and Maddy, standing inches apart and staring silently into each other's eyes, oblivious to everything else in the world around them. "But first, I'm going to have me a drink of real water."

He took his hat off, scooped up a quart or two from the rapidly spreading new pond and then drank before turning it over his head and letting the water soak him.

The other townspeople were reaching for their own six-shooters to back him up.

"There's not a whole lot of charity in this town, is there, Marshal?"

"Not for the likes of him." The marshal spat.

Slocum considered what to do. Without water, Marsh Campbell would die. But if he gave him the necessary water from his canteen, he would likely be shot down like a rabid dog. The mood of the crowd turned increasingly bilious. Slocum had seen lynch mobs that weren't this angry—or dangerous.

He spilled water over Campbell's lips. The hiss from the crowd sounded like a stepped-on rattler getting ready to strike. Slocum continued to drip water until some semblance of life had returned to the man.

"I said I'd pay for the water. How much for a canteen worth?" Slocum turned and stepped forward, his belly pressing into the barrel of the shotgun. His cold green eyes locked with the marshal's.

"Git outta town. Now, mister, now, if you know what's good for you."

Slocum slowly reached into his pocket, got a silver dollar and flipped it high into the air. It landed at the lawman's feet, kicking up a small dust cloud. Backing away, Slocum turned and felt the hairs rise on the back of his neck. He knew what was happening behind him. More than one of the men wanted to back-shoot him. Slocum slung his canteen, took the Appaloosa's reins and slowly led the horse with its burden away from the water barrel.

"Git outta Dehydration!" cried someone at the rear of the crowd. "And take him back to his kind."

Slocum didn't bother asking what "kind" that might be. He continued walking, and the feeling of danger subsided as he traversed the town from one end to the other in less than five minutes. Dehydration had once been three or four times the size it was now. From the number of water barrels placed along the street, he guessed this was the only source of water left for those who remained. The drought had been fierce this year, deadly fierce.

That didn't explain the treatment of the man who still flopped belly-down over his saddle. Slocum saw several more indications that the town's name had changed recently from Campbell to Dehydration. He began to wonder whether that change had come from a gallows humor generated by a lack of water or from a disaffection with the town's founding fathers.

As he reached the town limits he saw a newspaper fluttering in the night breeze. Slocum plucked it free from a patch of prickly pear cactus where it had gotten stuck and held it up. The light from town wasn't enough to read by, but the moon was rising and provided ample silvery illumination. As he walked, he scanned the headlines and other stories. What caught his attention was the reward of five thousand dollars for anyone who could return water to Dehydration.

Slocum chuckled when he saw that the mayor was putting out a call for any solution to the water problem. This would bring charlatans from throughout the West flocking in. He sobered when he saw a smaller article decrying ranchers with plenty of water who refused to share with their neighbors. No names were mentioned in the inch-long story, but Slocum didn't have to be a resident to know who was likely to be responsible.

"So you're keeping water from the town?" Slocum asked of his semiconscious travelling companion. "That must mean your spread's somewhere around here."

All he got in reply was a grunt. The man tried to lift his hand and point, but it was so weak that Slocum discounted it as pointing out any real direction. He kept walking, thinking of finding a place to bed down for the night when he saw a wood sign filled full of bullet holes. He dropped the reins and made his way across rocky ground to the sign and held it up.

"So the Circle C Ranch is in this direction? Let me guess. The C stands for Campbell." The way the sign had been used for target practice told Slocum that the towns-people had vented their anger more than once on this sign. Such venom caused him to wonder about the man slung over his saddle. If anyone in Dehydration thought Marsh Campbell was responsible for their water woes, they'd never have let him go free. In a coma or not, they would have strung him up.

All these little clues were adding up to what looked like a major feud. Slocum scrambled back to the Appaloosa and considered the shot-up sign and decided against bedding down quite yet. Less than a mile farther he came to a better marked road leading into the foothills. As he began trudg-ing up the steeper slope he noticed the bone-dry riverbed beside the road. It had been a long time since so much as a trickle of water had made its way down from higher eleva-tions, although Slocum had seen a snow pack on the high-est peaks in the Grand Tetons. He had to guess that there wasn't adequate runoff this year to keep the river wet.

Or to keep wet the town that had renamed itself Dehy-dration.

The more he saw of western Wyoming, the more he wanted to follow the buffalo south to greener, wetter pas-tures. West Texas could be mighty dry but central Mexico was always pleasant. Slocum vowed to deliver the young man he had rescued and then head south as soon as possi-ble. Or if he got enough water, pressing on to the Oregon coast presented a cool, damp alternative to the drought stretching out all around him. There'd be time to decide later. When he returned Marsh Campbell to his people.

Liberally sharing his single canteen of water with Marsh, he continued doggedly walking in the dark until he came to a narrow, high-walled canyon where the river had once flowed with such force that it had eaten notches in the hard granite. No water trickled now, but that didn't mean the area was devoid of life. Slocum spotted two alert sentries, one on each rim of the canyon silhouetted against the diamond-bright stars.

"Hello!" he called, waving to the men. "I've brought back Marsh Campbell. He was in an accident!" Slocum's words echoed along the barren canyon and were swallowed by distance. Both sentries disappeared, leaving him to wonder what he ought to do.

He shrugged it off and kept plodding along. It would be good when he could ride again. He wasn't used to putting so many miles under his boot soles, especially over such dry, hard ground.

Deeper in the canyon, he saw a dark wall looming. For a moment he thought the canyon had taken a sudden turn and he had missed it. Then he made out small details. A huge dam had been erected across the canyon and extended halfway up the sides.

Slocum pushed back his hat, mopped at his face and wondered at the structure. It had taken a powerful lot of effort to build something this large. Then he froze. The unmistakable sound of a six-shooter cocking came from his right.

"Evening," Slocum said, not turning. "You tell me how to get past that?" He pointed at the dam blocking the canyon.

"Is it true? Is that Marsh? If it isn't, I swear, I'll kill you where you stand. And him, too."

"You're not a very likable cuss, are you?" Slocum said, turning slowly. "Truth is, I haven't found anyone who's the least bit agreeable since I came on the accident."

"What happened?" The man speaking remained in shadow. Slocum had the feeling of others with him, lots of others, although he couldn't see them.